AuthorHouse™
1663 Liberty Drive
Bloomington, IN 47403
www.authorhouse.com
Phone: 1-800-839-8640

Published by AuthorHouse 12/28/2012

ISBN: 978-1-4772-9768-1 (sc)
*   978-1-4772-9769-8 (e)*

Library of Congress Control Number: 2012923301

Any people depicted in stock imagery provided by Thinkstock are models,
and such images are being used for illustrative purposes only.
Certain stock imagery © Thinkstock.

This book is printed on acid-free paper.

Because of the dynamic nature of the Internet, any web addresses or links contained in this book may have changed
since publication and may no longer be valid. The views expressed in this work are solely those of the author and do not
necessarily reflect the views of the publisher, and the publisher hereby disclaims any responsibility for them.

authorHOUSE®

Crime Scene Shooting (Trajectory)

Reconstruction

Workbook

2nd Edition

N. Leroy Parker

Table of Contents

Determining the bullet impact entrance angle to the horizontal plane
from the extended section of the dowel rod that was outside of the wall

This workbook is dedicated to my Crime Scene Co-workers and all the other Crime Scene Technicians and Investigators whom I have had the opportunity to work with, train and or learn from over the years that I have been doing crime scene processing, analysis and reconstruction.

Introduction

This workbook is designed to help the Crime Scene Analyst, Technician or Investigator in documenting the bullet holes and or indentations present at the scene. The documentation can be accomplished with overall, midrange and close-up photographs, rough sketches with the required measurement and notes.

The workbook is also designed to assist the Crime Scene Investigator in understanding the different ways of determining:

1.0   The upward *(inclined)* or downward *(sloped)* bullet impact angles to the horizontal plane and the horizontal bullet impact angles that would be needed to reconstruct the shooting incident.

2.0   The location of the muzzle of the gun at the time of the shooting

Upon finding the bullet impact angle(s) to the horizontal plane the Crime Scene Investigator can then determine the horizontal distance(s) below the path of the bullet and the distance(s) the bullet(s) traveled from the muzzle of the gun to the hole in the victim or object. These distances can be easily determined for any known or assumed muzzle height(s) based on the height of the shooter. Also, having the horizontal bullet impact angle the Crime Scene Investigator can determine the perpendicular distances from the muzzle of the gun to the surface with the bullet hole(s) and or indentation(s).

Potentially, very valuable investigative information can be developed through a trajectory or shooting reconstruction of the scene that would assist the Investigator in talking to a subject to determine if he or she is truthful in the sequence of events or the manner in which the incident took place. Specific information may be logically inferred if the Crime Scene Investigator is knowledgeable about trajectory or shooting reconstruction.

A trajectory or shooting reconstruction can, depending on the nature of the incident, lead to a determination of:

- The orientation and location of the individuals involved in the shooting incident *(subjects and victims)*
- The location of the shooter relative to a moving vehicle
- The sequence of the shots *(front windshield of a vehicle)* fired at the scene
- The location and or the position of objects in the path of the bullet(s) during the shooting incident

Thus a trajectory or shooting reconstruction can and do provide valuable information as to the truthfulness of the victim's and or subject's statement of the incident.

A trajectory or shooting reconstruction can be accomplished by the utilization of one or more of the following methods:

- Strings and dowels rods
- Scaled drawings
- Calculations using the trigonometric ratios
- Protractor with attached laser light or lasers alone

- Computers
- Total Station
- Animation

The emphasis of this workbook will be on the reconstruction of crime scene shooting incidents utilizing the following methods:
- The string method
- The scaled drawing method
- Calculations using the trigonometric ratios

  - The utilization of the Protractor with the attached laser will also be discussed but since its effectiveness is somewhat limited by the environmental factors *(too much light)* it is not always feasible to use it at an outdoor crime scene.
  - Utilization of the computer, the total station and animation will be left up to the individual student since there are so many crime scene sketching software on the market and all students may not be familiar with the same program

The workbook will explore the three above listed methods thus the student will have the opportunity to learn all three methods upon completion of the workshop.

The string method would involve at least two individuals to do the reconstruction and it is usually time consuming.

The scaled drawings can be done by a single individual and it is usually less time consuming than the string method.

The calculations using the trigonometric ratios are much faster and can be used to verify the accuracy of the two other methods.

The workbook also gives the student an opportunity to compare all three methods at the end of each set of assignments and determine which method is most accurate. Thus on completion of the workbook the student should know his or her margin of error for each set of assignments.

Thus if one uses several methods of determining the bullet impact entrance angle(s) to the horizontal plane and the horizontal bullet impact entrance angle(s) then one may use the average of the methods as the working angles. The difference between the average or mean and the largest or smallest angle may be used as a margin of error.

The location of the shooter should always be given as a range instead of a fixed location since the exact height of the muzzle of the gun would not be known but assumed in most cases depending on the height and orientation of the shooter at the time of the shooting.

Note: *The scene should always be documented with photographs, rough sketches with measurements and notes before attempting any reconstruction*

Curriculum Vitae

NAME: *N. Leroy Parker*

TITLE: Crime Laboratory Analyst Supervisor
- Crime Scene, Photography and Latent Prints

EDUCATION: Bachelor of Arts in Biology – 1974 from the University of the United States Virgin Islands, St. Thomas, U.S. V. I. Numerous Courses, Educational Conferences and Seminars on Crime Scene Procedures / Reconstruction, Shooting (Trajectory) Reconstruction, Bloodstain Pattern Analysis and Gunshot Residue Analysis that were presented by FDLE, the FBI Academy and other Agencies.

EXPERIENCE: Math and Science teacher in the United States Virgin Island Florida Department of Law Enforcement
- Crime Laboratory Analyst *(May 1980 to 1985)*
- Senior Crime Laboratory Analyst *(1985 to 1993)*
- Crime Laboratory Analyst Supervisor *(1993 to Present)*

SPECIALIZED TRAINING Certified by Fl. Dept. of Law Enforcement in the areas of:
AND CERTIFICATIONS:
- Crime Scene Processing / Analysis *(1980)*
- Bloodstain Pattern Analysis *(1982)*
- Gunshot Residue Analysis *(1982 to 1999)*

State Certified Instructor in Crime Scene Procedures
Currently teach classes / workshops for FDLE, the Daytona State College in Daytona Beach and other Agencies
- Crime Scene Procedures
- Bloodstain Pattern Analysis
- Shooting *(Trajectory)* Reconstruction

COURTROOM
EXPERIENCE: Testified in Circuit and Federal Courts in the state of Florida in excess of 500 times in the areas of:
Crime Scene Procedures / Analysis
Bloodstain Pattern Analysis
Shooting *(Trajectory)* Reconstruction
Gunshot Residue Analysis

PROFESSIONAL
AFFILIATIONS   International Association of Bloodstain Pattern Analysts and the Florida Division of the International Association for Identification

PUBLICATIONS: Presentations and workbooks on Crime Scene Procedures, Bloodstain Pattern Analysis and Shooting Reconstruction

What is required to complete the workbook?

The student will learn how to perform a presumptive test for lead, determine the impact angles and then determine the locations of the muzzle of the gun.

12 inch x 12inch wall with three bullet entrance holes and the corresponding exit holes *(two 12 inch 2 x 4 with 12 inch x 12 inch drywall attached to the edges)*

Three measuring tapes

3 or 6 cm stick-on tapes or any other stick-on tapes for the close-up photograph of the bullet holes

Camera with film or digital format for photographing the wall and the bullet holes and or indentations

Note pad and pen or pencil for rough sketches with measurements and notes

Several wooden dowel rods of different diameters

Dowels rods that can be attached to each other for long distances

Twelve (12) and six (6) inch transparent rules

Calipers for measuring the lengths and widths of the bullet holes and or indentations *(much easier to calculate the impact angles if the measurements of the lengths and widths of the holes are done in millimeters like blood spots)*

Scientific Calculator with the trigonometric ratios

Protractor with attached perpendicular base

Smart Level, Smart Laser, Smart Tool or Laser Trac etc.

Angle Finder(s)

Strings

Protractor with attached laser *(optional and very seldom used)*

Thumbtacks for anchoring the strings

Scotch tape and or clear packing tape for anchoring the strings

Tripod and a pistol grip for mounting the smart tools if necessary

Assignment #1 - Presumptive Test for Lead

Presumptive testing of suspected bullet holes and / or indentations for the presence of lead *(Sodium Rhodizonate)*

At the end of this training segment the student should be able to:

A. Identify the chemicals that are necessary to perform a presumptive test for lead

B. Correctly perform a presumptive test for lead

C. Correctly interpret the results of the presumptive test for lead

Chemicals:
- Saturated solution of Sodium Rhodizonate in distilled water
- Buffer solution of Sodium Bitartrate and Tartaric Acid in distilled water
- Diluted 5% solution of Hydrochloric Acid

Preparation of the Chemicals:
- Place a small amount of the Sodium Rhodizonate solution in a small beaker. Add a sufficient amount of the distilled water to make a saturated solution *(strong tea color)*. The solution is saturated if some of the sediment is observed at the bottom of the container after stirring the mixture.
- Dissolve 1.9 grams of the Sodium Bitartrate and 1.5 grams of the Tartaric Acid into 100 milliliters of the distilled water. Agitate or stir the mixture.
- Combine 5 milliliters of the concentrated Hydrochloric Acid with 95 milliliters of the distilled water. **Gently add the acid to the water.**

Performing the Test
Spraying of the reagents can be accomplished by using cans of compressed gas.
1.0 Spray the suspected bullet hole and the area around the hole with the saturated solution of the Sodium Rhodizonate in the distilled water
2.0 Next spray the suspected area with the buffer solution of the Sodium Bitartrate and the Tartaric Acid in the distilled water. A pink color would be indicative of lead but it must be confirmed with an additional procedure which is chemically specific for lead.
3.0 Apply a diluted *(5%)* solution of Hydrochloric Acid. A blue-violet color would indicate that lead is present.

Note: - *The Greiss test for partially burnt gun powder (Nitrites) should be first performed if a distance determination is to be done on the evidence with the bullet hole(s)*
- *Commercially prepared presumptive tests for lead are also available.*

Assignment #2 – Documentation of bullet holes

Training Objectives:
At the conclusion of this segment, the student should be able to:

- **A.** Take the necessary overall and midrange photographs of the front and rear of his or her assigned wall
- **B.** Determine what information should be placed on the 2, 3 or 6 cm or any other stick-on tapes *(Example – "hole #1a" for the entrance hole and "hole #1b" for the corresponding exit hole, case #, and date etc.)*
- **C.** Determine how and where the stick-on tapes should be placed on the wall to document each bullet entrance and corresponding exit holes in the wall
- **D.** Take the necessary midrange photographs with the stick-on tapes to show the relationship of the labeled bullet entrance and exit holes in the wall
- **E.** Take the necessary close-up photographs of each bullet entrance and corresponding exit holes with the stick-on tapes
- **F.** Make rough sketches to show the shape of the wall and the relative locations of each bullet entrance and corresponding exit holes in the wall
- **G.** Determine the height and horizontal distances to the *center* of each bullet entrance and corresponding exit holes in the wall
- **H.** Describe each bullet entrance and corresponding exit holes in the wall

Documentation of the wall and the three bullet entrance and corresponding exit holes

2A1. - Overall photographs of the wall with the bullet holes

Overall photographs of the wall

Front of the wall

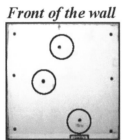

Photograph to show *the locations* of the three (3) bullet entrance holes in the wall

Rear of the wall

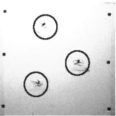

Photograph to show *the locations* of the three (3) bullet exit holes in the wall

Top of the wall

Photograph to show *the top* of the wall

Side of the wall

Photograph to show *one of the sides* of the wall

2A2. **- Midrange photographs of the three bullet entrance and exit holes with a measuring tape *(rule)* to show *the height of each bullet hole***

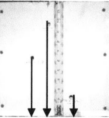

Photograph to show *the height of the center* of each bullet entrance hole

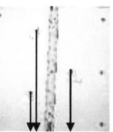

Photograph to show *the height of the center* of each bullet exit hole

- Midrange photographs of the three entrance and exit holes with a measuring tape *(rule)* to show *the horizontal distance of each bullet hole*

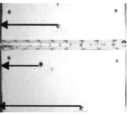

Photograph to show *the horizontal distance from the center* of each bullet entrance hole to the *left* edge of the wall

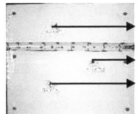

Photograph to show *the horizontal distance from the center* of each bullet exit hole to the **right** edge of the wall *(Only if you rotated your wall 180 degrees)*

2A3. **Close-up photographs of the three (3) bullet entrance and exit holes**
Note:
- *Each bullet entrance and exit hole should be photographed as discovered*
- *Write the necessary info. (hole#, case#, date etc.) on each stick-on tape*
- *Place a stick-on tape with the necessary information below each bullet hole*
- *Each stick-on tape should be placed the right way up (horizontally)*
- *Photograph each bullet hole separately*
- *The camera lens should be parallel to the surface with the bullet holes*
- *Each hole with a stick-on tape should be in the center of the photograph*
    . Maximize (largest possible) the size of the image in the photograph

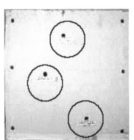

Photograph to show *the stick-on tape* below each bullet entrance hole

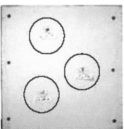

Photograph to show *the stick-on tape* below each bullet exit hole

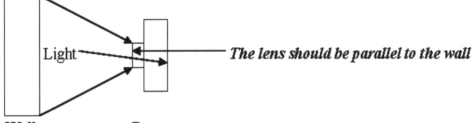

Light —

The lens should be parallel to the wall

Wall   **Camera**

Diagram showing *the position of the camera lens* relative to the wall

13

2A4. **Other photographs of the wall** *(for this assignment only)* **that should be taken after documenting the bullet holes**

Note:

Place the three (3) best fitting dowel rods through the bullet entrance and corresponding exit holes

Horizontal bullet impact angles

Photograph to show *the top view* of the wall with the dowel rods in place

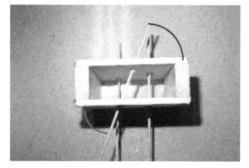

Note:

*This view shows **the horizontal bullet impact entrance angle** at the bottom and **the horizontal bullet impact exit angle** at the top of the wall. The view also shows the orientation of the dowel rods in the center of the wall. Note that some of the sections of the rods in the wall are longer because of the different horizontal impact angles.*

Impact angles to the horizontal plane

Photograph to show *one of the edges* of the wall with the dowel rods in place

Note:

*This view shows **the bullet impact entrance angles to the horizontal plane** on the right and **the bullet impact exit angles to the horizontal plane** on the left side of the photograph of the wall. The bullet impact entrance and the corresponding exit angles are the same because there was no deflection of the bullets through the wall.*

2B1. Documentation of the wall and the three (3) bullet entrance and corresponding exit holes

Rough sketches

Make rough proportional sketches of the wall to show the locations of the bullet holes

      a. Maximize the size of your sketches on the paper

      b. Draw the best straight lines that you can **_without a ruler_**

      c. Sketch the walls as they appear *(i.e. rectangular, square or round etc.)*

      d. Place the bullet holes in the approximate locations on your rough sketch as they appear on the wall

      e. Draw the bullet holes the way they appear *(round, oval or non-descript etc.)*   ***Complete your rough sketch here***

Front of the wall

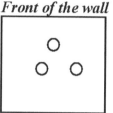

Rough sketch showing *the approximate locations* of the bullet **entrance** holes in the square wall   ***Complete your rough sketch here***

Back of the wall

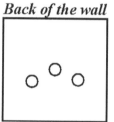

Rough sketch showing *the approximate locations* of the bullet **exit** holes in the square wall   ***Side of the wall***   ***Complete your rough sketch here***

Rough sketch showing the ***rectangular edge*** of the wall

      Top of the wall   *Complete your **rough** sketch here*

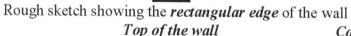

Rough sketch showing the *top rectangular view* of the wall with the edges of the 2 x 4s

2B2. Documentation of the wall and the three (3) bullet entrance and corresponding exit holes

Measurements

Overall measurements
Measure the length and width of the wall (Note: *It is ALWAYS much easier to do all of your measurements in inches rather than feet and inches*)

a. Bullet entrance holes *(Enter your results in the table on page 18)*
- Measure the height of each bullet hole
- Measure the horizontal distance from the left edge of the wall to each bullet hole
Note: The measurements should be done from the center of each bullet hole

12 inches   12 inches

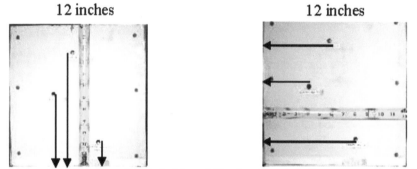

Photographs showing *the height* and *the horizontal distance* to the left edge or reference side for each bullet entrance hole in the wall

- Measure the length and width of each bullet entrance hole *(Enter the results in the table on page 18)*

*Note: These measurements should be done in **millimeters** to make the calculations (if necessary) of the bullet impact entrance angles much easier*

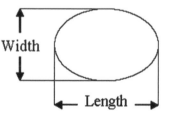

Diagram showing *how to measure* the length and width of each bullet entrance hole

16

Measurements continued

Note: *These measurements should also be done from the **center** of each bullet hole*

b. **Bullet exit holes** (*Enter your results in the table on page 18*)
- Measure the height of each bullet exit hole
- Measure the horizontal distance from the **right** edge of the wall to each bullet exit hole (*Note: Only if you rotated your wall 180 degrees*)

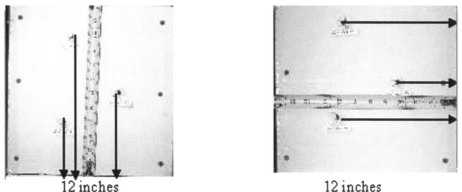

12 inches   12 inches
- Measure the length and width of each bullet exit hole if possible

*These measurements if possible should also be done in **millimeters***

c. **Bullet indentations**
- Measure the length of the bullet indentation in millimeters
- Measure the width of the bullet indentation in millimeters

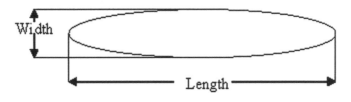

The impact angle of a bullet that made the indentation in the surface could be determined from *the width to length ratio* of the indentation

Example: *Width of the bullet indentation = 3 millimeters*
                  Length of the bullet indentation = 15 millimeters

Divide the width by the length
Example: 3 mm / 15 mm = 0.200
Using the *sine tables* in the rear of the book to find which angle = 0.200
That bullet impact angle is approximately **11.5 degrees**

Data collected from the three (3) bullet entrance and corresponding exit holes in the wall

Record the locations of the six bullet holes in the wall in the two tables below

<u>Locations of the (3) three bullet entrance holes</u>

Entrance bullet holes	Height of the entrance holes ↓	Horizontal distances to the left edge ←
#1		
#2		
#3		

<u>Locations of the (3) three corresponding bullet exit holes</u>

Exit bullet holes	Height of the exit holes ↓	Horizontal distances to the right edge →
#1		
#2		
#3		

Impact angles from the width to length ratios

Note: The entrance impact angle in the direction of travel of the bullets that made the three holes in the wall may be determined by dividing the width by the corresponding length of each bullet hole and then determining the arc sine of the result of each answer from your scientific calculator or the sine tables that is provided at the back of this work book (Not necessary for this assignment – Only used where there is no secondary bullet impact site / hole)

Entrance bullet holes	Width of the bullet holes	Length of the bullet holes	Width / Length (/ = divided by)	Angle-sine tables (arc sine)
#1				
#2				
#3				

Assignment #3 – Bullet impact entrance angles

Training objects:
At the conclusion of this segment, the student should be able to:

    A. *Determine the bullet impact angles to the horizontal plane using:*
- A Smart Level, Smart Laser and / or Laser Trac etc.
- An Angle Finder
- A Protractor
- Scaled Drawings
- Calculations

    B. *Determine the horizontal bullet impact angles using:*
- A Protractor
- Scaled Drawings
- Calculations

1.0 The bullet impact angle to the horizontal plane
(The sloped *(downward)* or inclined *(upward)* path of the bullet)
This is the **angle** *that would be needed to determine the location of the muzzle of the gun and the shooter for any given muzzle height*

2.0 The horizontal bullet impact angle

Determination of the above impact bullet entrance angles of the bullet holes in the wall by the following methods:

3A1 and 3A2   The shape of the bullet entrance hole
(Width to length ratio – The orientation of the hole is <u>very</u> *important)*

3A3   Protractor

3A4   Smart Tool, Smart Level, Smart Laser or Laser Trac etc.)

3A5   Angle Finder

3A6   Scaled Drawings

3A7   Calculations

3A8   Computer *(if available)*

Determining the bullet impact entrance angles

3A1. Shape of the bullet entrance hole
(Bullet impact angle to the surface in the direction of travel of the bullet)
The _accuracy_ of the bullet impact angles depends to a great extent on the precision of your measurements

- *Usually better for angles less than 70 degrees*
- *The determined bullet impact angle is the **downward** or **upward** angle if the impacted surface is in a **horizontal plane** and the **horizontal bullet impact angle** if the impacted surface is in a **vertical plane***
- *Normally used when there is **no secondary** bullet impact site(s) or exit hole(s)*
- *Used extensively in Bloodstain Pattern Analysis*

1.0 Circular
Indicative of a bullet impact angle of approximately 90 degrees

2.0 Oval
Indicative of a bullet impact angle that is less than 90 degrees
The more oval the shape of the bullet hole, the smaller the bullet impact angle

3.0 Nondescript
Indicative of an impact angle that was made by damaged bullet which first penetrated another object. Also indicative of a bullet impact made in the hard plastic in some vehicles
It is usually very difficult to determine the bullet impact angle(s) unless there is a second bullet impact site

4.0 Rectangular
Indicative of an impact angle made by a tumbling bullet that penetrated another object and or a ricocheted bullet
It is usually also very difficult to determine the bullet impact angle(s) unless there is a second bullet impact site

Determining the bullet impact entrance angles

3A2. Shape of the bullet indentation *(Bullet impact angle to the surface in the direction of travel of the bullet)*

The determined bullet impact angle is the **downward** *or* **upward angle** *if the impacted surface is in* **a horizontal plane** *and the* **horizontal bullet impact angle** *if the bullet impacted surface is* **in a vertical plane**

1.0   Circular
Indicative of an impact made by a bullet that struck a surface at 90 degrees without penetrating that surface
Example: A bullet impacting a concrete surface at 90 degrees

2.0   Oval
Indicative of an impact made by a bullet that was deflected off the surface of a vehicle or similar object
The bullet impact angle is usually less than 15 degrees
Example: An indentation on the side of a vehicle that was made by a bullet

3.0   Nondescript
Indicative of an impact made by a damaged bullet that struck a surface without penetrating that surface
This bullet impact angle is usually very difficult to determine
Example: A bullet that struck a surface without penetrating the surface or was deflected off of a surface after penetrating a victim or an object

4.0   Rectangular
Indicative of an impact made by a tumbling bullet that struck a surface without penetrating the surface
Example: A tumbling bullet impacting a wooden surface at 90 degrees

Determining the bullet impact entrance angles
(Using only the width to length ratios of the bullet entrance holes)

Caution!!!

Extreme care must be taken when determining the bullet impact entrance angles in drywalls or other similar objects where there are bullet entrance holes and corresponding exit holes. Both the bullet entrance and exit holes should always be used to obtain the most accurate bullet impact angle.

The best fitting dowel rod should be placed through both the bullet entrance and the corresponding exit holes and not through the bullet entrance hole alone.

Do not use a dowel that is too large as it might damage the shape of the hole.

Do not remove the section of the wall or object with the bullet entrance hole and then try to determine the bullet impact entrance angle from this bullet hole by using the width to length ratio of the bullet hole

There is usually a bevel made by the bullet as it enters the drywall at an angle less than 90 degrees (usually more obvious between 50 and 70 degrees). Placing the dowel rod on the beveled surface to determine the bullet impact entrance angle may result in an error of up to about 10 degrees

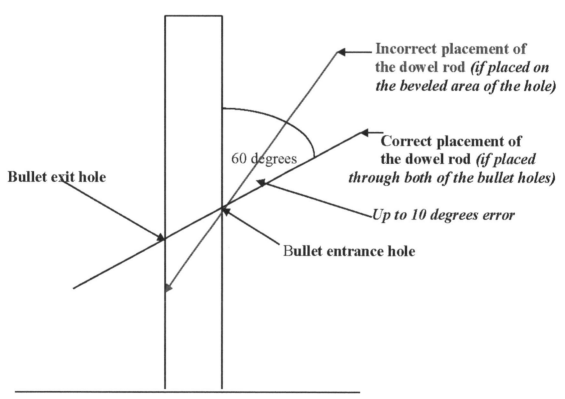

Determining the bullet impact entrance angles

(Bullet impact angles to the horizontal plane and the horizontal bullet impact angles)

3A3. Protractor *(Enter your results for this section in the tables on pages 71 to 73)*

The reference point *(Center of the base of the Protractor)* should be at the center of the base line to obtain the most accurate results

(To avoid any errors the legs or the rule at the base of the Protractor should be removed before using it to measure any of the bullet impact angles in the wall)

Examples of the wrong Protractors to use to obtain the best bullet impact angles

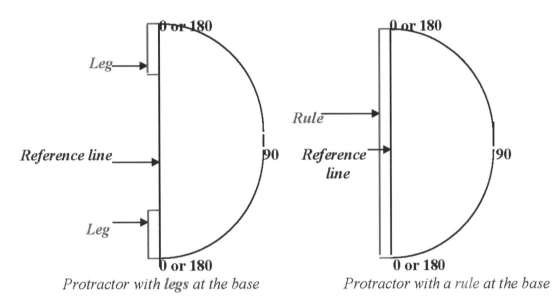

Protractor with **legs** at the base   Protractor with a **rule** at the base

Example of a correct Protractor to use to obtain the best (most accurate) bullet impact angles

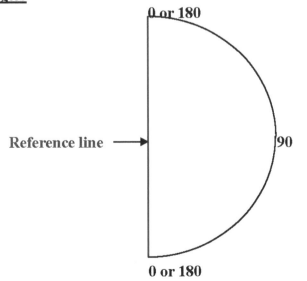

Protractor *without* any **legs or rule** at the base

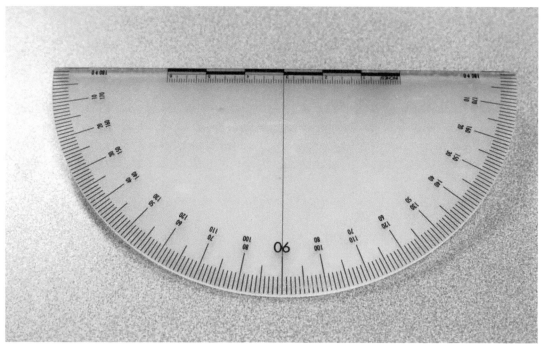

Photograph of a **Protractor** that could also be used with the application of the dowel rod in the bullet entrance and corresponding exit holes or the string that is attached to center of the blood spot on the bloodstained surface.

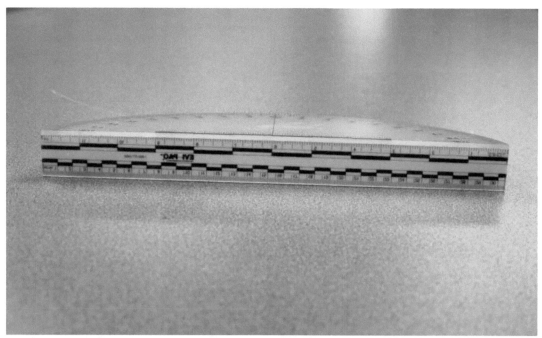

Side view of the **_base_** of the above **Protractor** that would make it possible for the Protractor to be held perpendicular or at 90 degrees to the surface to determine the impact angles of the paths of the bullets that made the bullet entrance and corresponding exit holes or the blood spots that impacted the surface in question

Determining the bullet impact entrance angles

3A3. Protractor continued

. **Could be used to measure both the *bullet impact angles to the horizontal plane* and *horizontal bullet* impact angles (Note: *The wall should be plumb)* Walls**

Use of the *top* of the dowel rod as the reference line to determine **the downward impact angle of 20 degrees** to the horizontal plane **(Protractor held *VERTICAL*)**

Use of the *center* of the dowel rod as the reference line to determine **the upward impact angle of 10 degrees** to the horizontal plane **(Protractor held *VERTICAL*)**

Use of the *center* of the dowel rod as the reference line to determine ***the horizontal bullet impact angle of 80 degrees to the right*** when facing the wall ***(Protractor held HORIZONTAL)***

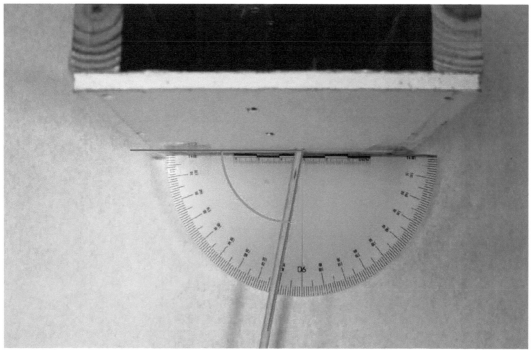

Use of the *right side* of the dowel rod as the reference line to determine ***the horizontal bullet impact angle of 80 degrees to the left*** when facing the wall ***(Protractor held HORIZONTAL)***

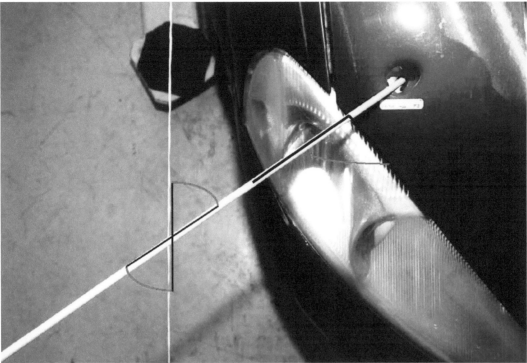

The **horizontal bullet impact angle** to the headlamp lens and to a section of the *rectangular shaped string* that was placed around the vehicle could be measured with a Protractor

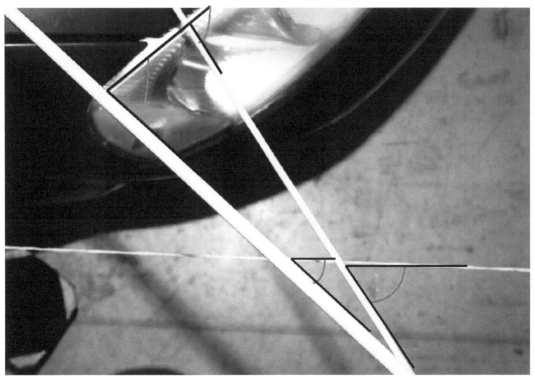

The **horizontal bullet impact angles** to the lens and to a section of the *rectangular shaped string* that was placed around the vehicle could be measured with a Protractor

Determining the bullet impact entrance angles
(Bullet impact angles to the horizontal plane)

3A4. Smart Level, Smart Laser or Laser Trac *(Enter your results in the tables on pages 71 to 73)*

Could be obtained as a 10 inch, 2 foot (24 inches) or a 4 foot (48 inches) level

Could only be used to determine *the bullet impact angles to the horizontal plane*

The angles obtained should be readable to the nearest tenth of a degree

The bullet impact angle to the horizontal plane *is the upward or downward angle to the horizontal line that is drawn at the height of the bullet entrance or exit hole*

Could also be used on the extended dowel rod from curve surfaces *(the curved sides of vehicles)* and on non-plumb surfaces

The bullet impact angle that would be needed later to calculate or determine the location of the muzzle of the gun

Smart Laser

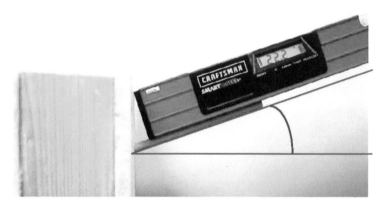

Use of a *Smart Laser* to determine *the downward bullet impact angle of 22.2 degrees to the horizontal plane*

Smart Level

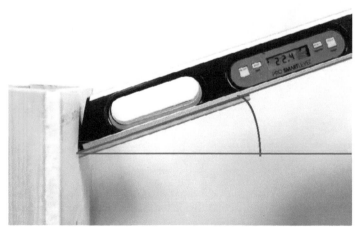

Use of a *Smart Level* to determine *the downward bullet impact angle of 22.4 degrees to the horizontal plane*

Smart Laser

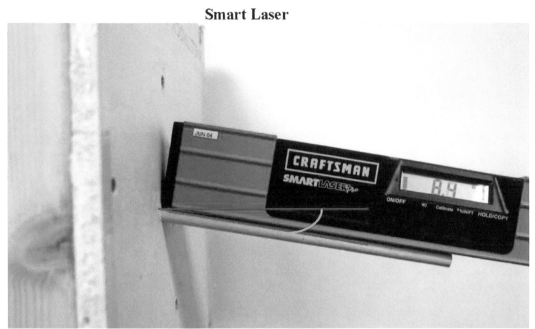

Use of a *Smart Laser* to determine *the upward bullet impact angle of 8.4 degrees to the horizontal plane.* The arrow on the right next to the degree symbol always points upwards.

Smart Level

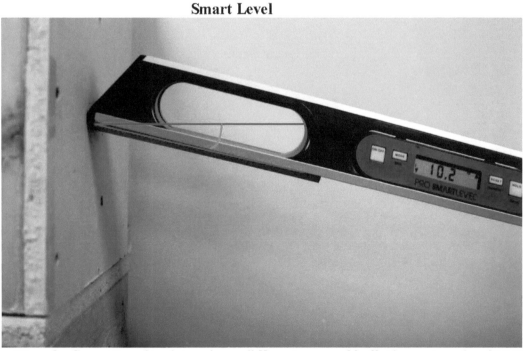

Use of a *Smart Level* to determine a different *upward bullet impact angle of 10.2 degrees to the horizontal plane.* The arrow head with the line on the left of the numbers always points downward.

Laser Trac

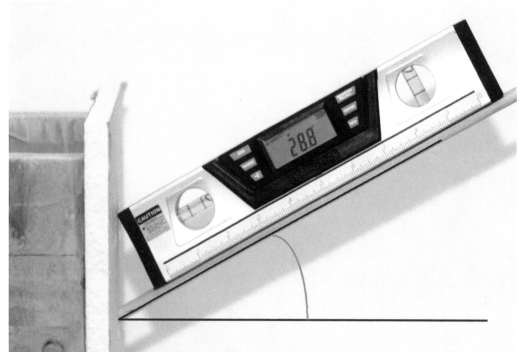

Use of a *Laser Trac* to determine *the **downward bullet impact angle of 28.8 degrees to the horizontal plane.** The downward arrow below the angle symbol and the angle symbol at the top left corner of the digital angle determines how the impact angle is measured.*

Laser Trac

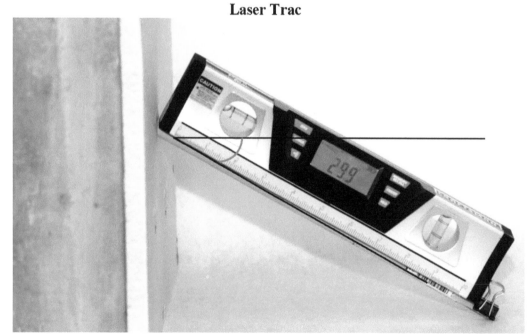

Use of a *Laser Trac* to determine *the **upward bullet impact angle of 29.9 degrees to the horizontal plane.** The upward arrow above the angle symbol and the symbol at the top left corner of the digital angle determines how the impact angle is measured.*

Determining the bullet impact entrance angles
(Bullet impact angles to the horizontal plane)

3A5. Angle Finder *(Enter your results in the tables on pages 71 to 73)*

. Could only be used to determine *the bullet impact angle to the horizontal plane*
- *The bullet impact angle to the horizontal plane is the upward or downward angle to the horizontal line that is drawn at the height of the entrance or exit hole*
- **Could be used on the extended dowel rod from curve surfaces** *(the curved sides of vehicles)* **and on non-plumb surfaces**
- *This is the bullet impact angle that would be needed later to calculate or determine the location of the muzzle of the gun*

Use of an *Angle Finder* to determine the *downward bullet impact angle* of *approximately 22 degrees to the horizontal plane* which is measured from the top of dowel rod on the **right** side of the zero line

Use of an *Angle Finder* to determine *the upward bullet impact angle of approximately 9 degrees to the horizontal plane* which is measured from the bottom of the dowel rod on the **left** side of the zero line

Determining the bullet impact entrance angles
(Bullet impact angles to horizontal plane and or the horizontal bullet impact angles)

3A6. Scaled Drawings
- Could be used to determine the bullet impact angles to the horizontal plane and the horizontal bullet impact angles

Place the best fitting dowel rod through each of the bullet entrance and corresponding exit holes

Mark the dowel rods on the entrance and exit sides of the wall for each pair of bullet holes

Remove the dowel rods and measure the distance between the two marks for each pair of bullet holes. **Enter your result for hole #1 on pages 36 and 65, hole #2 on pages 38 and 67 and hole #3 on pages 40 and 69.** This distance would represent the distance the bullet traveled through the wall for each pair of bullet entrance and corresponding exit holes

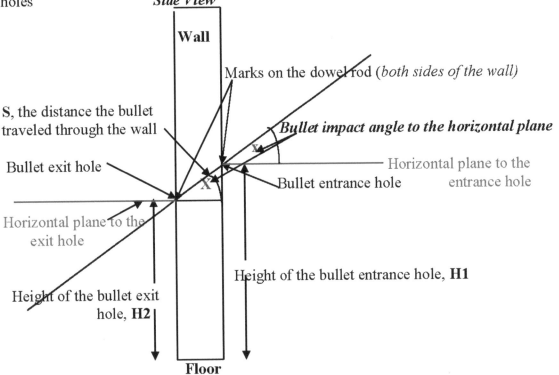

Obtain the following information from the measurements that were taken earlier:

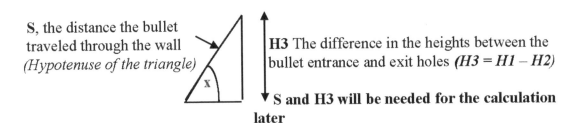

S, the distance the bullet traveled through the wall *(Hypotenuse of the triangle)*

H3 The difference in the heights between the bullet entrance and exit holes *(H3 = H1 – H2)*

S and H3 will be needed for the calculation later

Determining the bullet impact entrance angles

3A6. Scaled drawings continued

Information required for drawing the scaled diagram to determine *the bullet impact angle to the horizontal plane*
Example:

- Height of the bullet entrance hole, **H1**   = **9 inches**
- Height of the bullet exit hole, **H2**   = **6 inches**
- Difference in the heights, **H3 (H1 – H2)**   = **(9 – 6) inches = 3 inches**
- Distance the bullet traveled through the wall, S   = **5 inches**

Complete the triangle from the above information:
    Note: the best scale should be chosen to maximize your scaled diagram

Instructions for drawing the right-angled triangle:
   1.   Draw line AB to represent the difference in heights, H3 = 3 inches
   2.   From B draw line BC perpendicular (90 degrees) to line AB
   3.   From A determine where line AC (S = the distance the bullet traveled through the wall) should intersect line BC
   4.   Draw line AC to complete the right angled triangle
   5.   Measure angle C or ACB with your protractor *(Angle C or ACB is the bullet impact angle to the horizontal plane)*

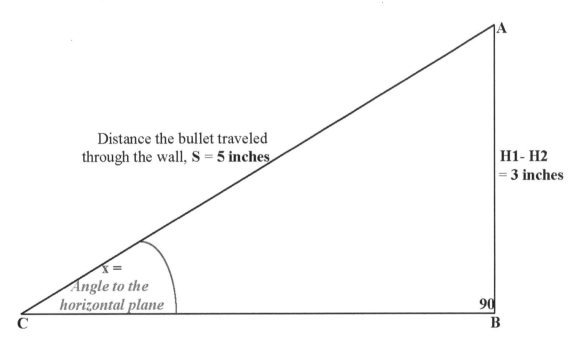

Determining the bullet impact entrance angles

3A6. Scaled drawings continued
Information required for drawing the scaled diagram to determine the horizontal bullet impact angle

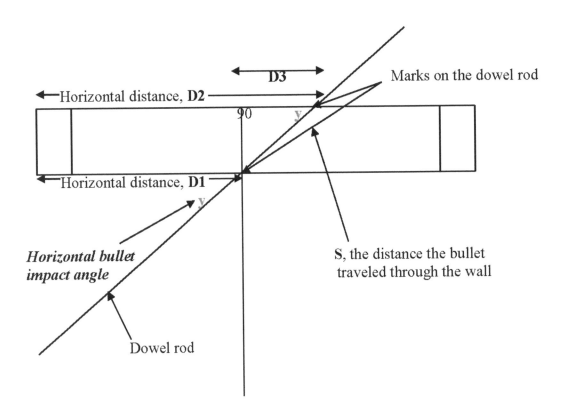

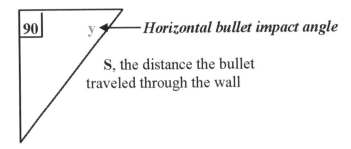

D3, the difference in the horizontal distances

Determining the bullet impact entrance angles

3A6. Scaled drawings continued

Information required for drawing the scaled diagram to determine the horizontal bullet impact angle

Example:

- Distance of the bullet entrance hole, **D1**   **= 5 inches**
- Distance of the bullet exit hole, **D2**   **= 8 inches**
- Difference in the distances, **D3 = (D2 – D1)**   **= (8 – 5) inches = 3 inches**
- Distance the bullet traveled through the wall, S   **= 5 inches**

Complete the triangle from the above information:
Note: the best scale should be chosen to maximize your scaled diagram

Instructions for drawing the right-angled triangle:

1.0   Draw line DE to represent the difference in distances, D3 = 3 inches
2.0   From D draw line DF perpendicular (90 degrees) to line DE
3.0   From E determine where line EF (S = 5 inches, the distance the bullet traveled through the wall) should intersect line DF
4.0   Draw line EF to complete the right angled triangle
5.0   Measure angle E or DEF with your protractor *(This angle is your horizontal bullet impact angle)*

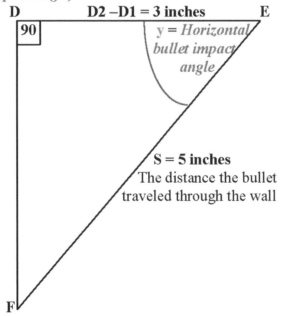

Determining the bullet impact entrance angles

3A6.   Scaled drawings continued

Determine the *two* (2) bullet impact angles for the three bullet entrance and corresponding exit holes in your wall by scaled drawings *(PLEASE see examples on pages 33 to 35)*

Bullet Hole #1

Retrieve the information from your table on __page 18__ *to determine:*
a. __The bullet impact angle to the horizontal plane:__
Information
- *Height of the bullet entrance hole, H1*   =
- *Height of the bullet exit hole, H2*   =
- *Difference in the heights, H3*   =
- *Distance the bullet traveled through the wall, S*   =

Instructions:
- *Draw line AB to represent the difference in the heights, H3*
- *From B draw line BC perpendicular (90 degrees) to line AB*
- *From A determine where line AC should intersect line BC*
- *Draw line AC to complete the right-angled triangle ABC*
- *__Measure angle C or ACB with your protractor__*

b.   __The horizontal bullet impact angle:__
Information
- *Horizontal distance of the bullet entrance hole, D1*   =
- *Horizontal distance of the bullet exit hole, D2*   =
- *Difference in the horizontal distances, D3*   =
- *Distance the bullet traveled through the wall, S*   =

Instructions:
- *Draw line DE to represent the difference in the horizontal distances, D3*
- *From D draw line DF perpendicular (90 degrees) to line DE*
- *From E determine where line EF should intersect line DF*
- *Draw line EF to complete the right-angled triangle DEF*
- *__Measure angle E or DEF with your protractor__*

Determining the bullet impact entrance angles

Draw your scaled drawings for bullet hole #1 below (Enter your results in the tables on pages 71 to 73)

Determining the bullet impact entrance angles

3A6.   Scaled drawings continued

Determine the *two* (2) bullet impact angles for the three bullet entrance and corresponding exit holes in your wall by scaled drawings *(PLEASE see examples on pages 33 to 35)*

Bullet Hole #2

Retrieve the information from your table on __page 18__ *to determine:*
a. __The bullet impact angle to the horizontal plane:__
Information
- *Height of the bullet entrance hole, H1*   =
- *Height of the bullet exit hole, H2*   =
- *Difference in the heights, H3*   =
- *Distance the bullet traveled through the wall, S*   =

Instructions:
- *Draw line AB to represent the difference in heights, H3*
- *From B draw line BC perpendicular (90 degrees) to line AB*
- *From A determine where line AC should intersect line BC*
- *Draw line AC to complete the right-angled triangle ABC*
- ***Measure angle C or ACB with your protractor***

b.   __The horizontal bullet impact angle:__
Information
- *Horizontal distance of the bullet entrance hole, D1*   =
- *Horizontal distance of the bullet exit hole, D2*   =
- *Difference in the horizontal distances, D3*   =
- *Distance the bullet traveled through the wall, S*   =

Instructions:
- *Draw line DE to represent the difference in the horizontal distances, D3*
- *From D draw line DF perpendicular (90 degrees) to line DE*
- *From E determine where line EF should intersect line DF*
- *Draw line EF to complete the right-angled triangle DEF*
- ***Measure angle E or DEF with your protractor***

Determining the bullet impact entrance angles

Draw your scaled drawings for bullet hole #2 below (Enter your results in the tables on pages 71 to 73)

Determining the bullet impact entrance angles

3A6.   Scaled drawings continued

Determine the *two* (2) bullet impact angles for the three bullet entrance and corresponding exit holes in your wall by scaled drawings *(PLEASE see examples on pages 33 to 35)*

Bullet Hole #3

Retrieve the information from your table on **page 18** *to determine:*
a. *The bullet impact angle to the horizontal plane:*
Information
- *Height of the bullet entrance hole, H1*   =
- *Height of the bullet exit hole, H2*   =
- *Difference in the heights, H3*   =
- *Distance the bullet traveled through the wall, S*   =

Instructions:
- *Draw line AB to represent the difference in heights, H3*
- *From B draw line BC perpendicular (90 degrees) to line AB*
- *From A determine where line AC should intersect line BC*
- *Draw line AC to complete the right-angled triangle ABC*
- ***Measure angle C or ACB with your protractor***

b.   *The horizontal bullet impact angle:*
Information
- *Horizontal distance of the bullet entrance hole, D1*   =
- *Horizontal distance of the bullet exit hole, D2*   =
- *Difference in the horizontal distances, D3*   =
- *Distance the bullet traveled through the wall, S*   =

Instructions:
- *Draw line DE to represent the difference in the horizontal distances, D3*
- *From D draw line DF perpendicular (90 degrees) to line DE*
- *From E determine where line EF should intersect line DF*
- *Draw line EF to complete the right-angled triangle DEF*
- ***Measure angle E or DEF with your protractor***

Determining the bullet impact entrance angles

Draw your scaled drawings for bullet hole #3 below (Enter your results in the tables on pages 71 to 73)

Math (Geometry) Review
Training Objectives:

At the conclusion of this segment, the student would be able to:

1.0 Demonstrate a working knowledge of how to name the sides of a right angled triangle relative to the angle in question

2.0 Demonstrate a working knowledge of how complimentary and supplementary angles could be used in determining the unknown angle(s) of a right angled triangle

3.0 Demonstrate a working knowledge of the use of the Pythagorean Theorem and how it could be used in the reconstruction of shooting incidents

4.0 Demonstrate a working knowledge of the use of the Trigonometric Ratios *(Sine, Cosine and Tangent)* and how they could be used in the reconstruction of shooting incidents

5.0 Demonstrate an understanding of the basic mathematical principles;
   a. It is mathematically correct to cross-multiply in equations
   Example if 2 = 6 / 3 then 2 x 3 = 6
   b. It is mathematically correct to multiply or divide both sides of the equation by the same number or unknown such as a letter "a"
   Example if 2 = 6 / 3 then 2 x 3 = 6 / 3 x3
   Example if 2 x 3 = 6 then 2 x 3 / 2 = 6 / 2
   c. It is mathematically correct to add or subtract the same number or unknown such as a letter "a" to or from each side of the equation
   Example if 2 + 4 = 6 then 2 + 4 – 4 = 6 - 4
   Example if 2 + 4 = 6 then 2 + 4 + 2 = 6 + 2

6.0 Demonstrate a working knowledge of how to solve for the unknown by making it the subject of the equation in order to easily solve for the unknown
   Example if 2 = 6 / a
   2 x a = 6
   2 x a / 2 = 6 / 2
   Or a = 6 / 2

7.0 Demonstrate a working knowledge of the mathematics that would be used to determine the impact angles by calculation

8.0 Demonstrate a working knowledge of the mathematics that would be used to determine the location of the muzzle of the weapon for any given muzzle height
   The muzzle height of a gun usually varies between 4 and 5 feet for an average height person (5.75 to 6.25 feet) in an upright position.

Math Review

Angles

Definition: *An angle is the figure formed by two straight lines that meet*

Angles are measured quantitatively by defining a unit angle as being *1/180* of a straight line

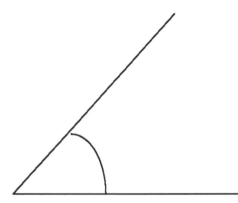

An <u>acute</u> angle – *Less than 90 degrees*

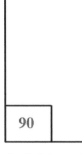

A <u>right</u> angle – *Always 90 degrees*

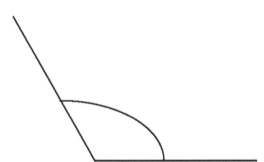

An <u>obtuse</u> angle – *Greater than 90 degrees or a right angle but less than 180 degrees*

A <u>straight</u> angle – *Always 180 degrees*

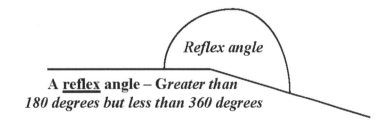

A <u>reflex</u> angle – *Greater than 180 degrees but less than 360 degrees*

Math Review continued

Relationship between angles

1.0   **Two angles are complimentary if their sum total** *(is equal to)* **90 degrees**

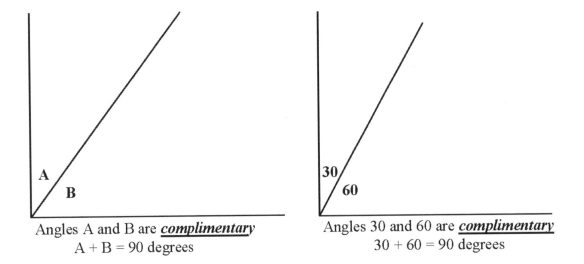

Angles A and B are <u>*complimentary*</u>
A + B = 90 degrees

Angles 30 and 60 are <u>*complimentary*</u>
30 + 60 = 90 degrees

Two angles are supplementary if their sum total *(is equal to)* **= 180 degrees**

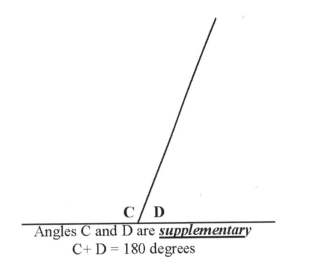
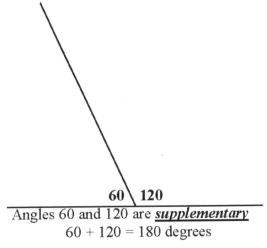

Angles C and D are <u>*supplementary*</u>
C+ D = 180 degrees

Angles 60 and 120 are <u>*supplementary*</u>
60 + 120 = 180 degrees

Math Review continued

Intersecting straight lines

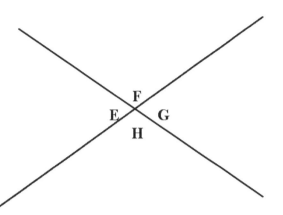

Angles E and G are equal *(Vertically opposite angles)*
Angles F and H are equal *(Vertically opposite angles)*
Angles E and F and angles E and H are **supplementary** *(Their sum = 180 degrees)*
Angles G and F and angles G and H are **supplementary** *(Their sum = 180 degrees)*

Parallel lines intersected by a straight line

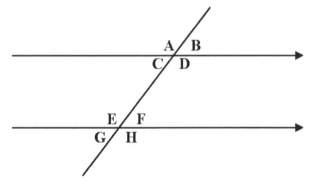

Angles A, D, E and H are all equal *(Vertically opposite angles)*
Determine which other angles are equal *(Vertically opposite angles)*

Angles A and B, B and D, D and C, C and A are **supplementary**
Determine which angles in the group G, E, F and H are **supplementary**

Angles A and G, A and F are **supplementary**
Determine which angles from the group are **supplementary to B, C and D**
Clue: *Replace the letters with numbers* (Example: let A = 120 then B = 60)

Math Review continued

Practice Problems:

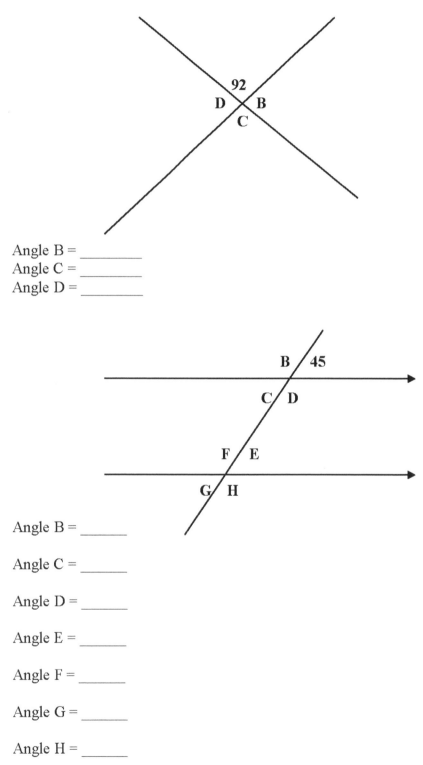

Angle B = _____
Angle C = _____
Angle D = _____

Angle B = _____

Angle C = _____

Angle D = _____

Angle E = _____

Angle F = _____

Angle G = _____

Angle H = _____

Math Review continued

Parallel lines intersected by a straight line

Assume the two sides of the wall are the parallel lines and the arrow is the path of a bullet that penetrated the wall

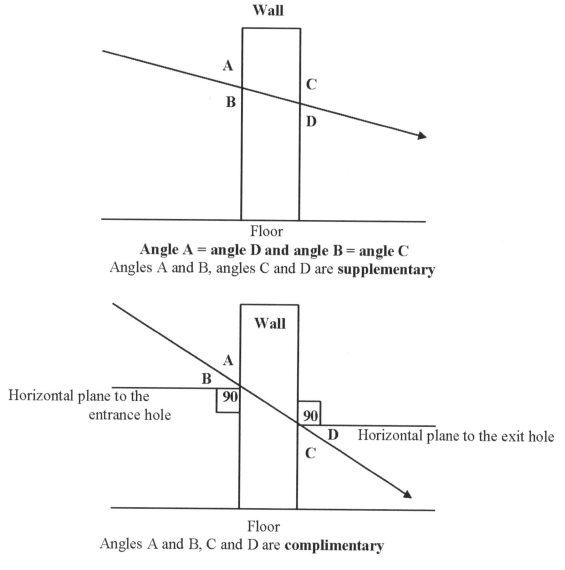

Wall

A

C

B

D

Floor

Angle A = angle D and angle B = angle C
Angles A and B, angles C and D are **supplementary**

Wall

A

B

Horizontal plane to the
entrance hole

90

90

D   Horizontal plane to the exit hole

C

Floor
Angles A and B, C and D are **complimentary**

Angle A = angle C and angle B = angle D

Angles A and C represent **angles to the vertical plane**
Angles B and D represent **angles to the horizontal plane**

Angle A + angle B + the right angle = **180 degrees** *(Angles on a straight line)*
Angle C + angle D + the right angle = **180 degrees** *(Angles on a straight line)*

Math Review continued

Practice Problems:

Explain how you determine the angles

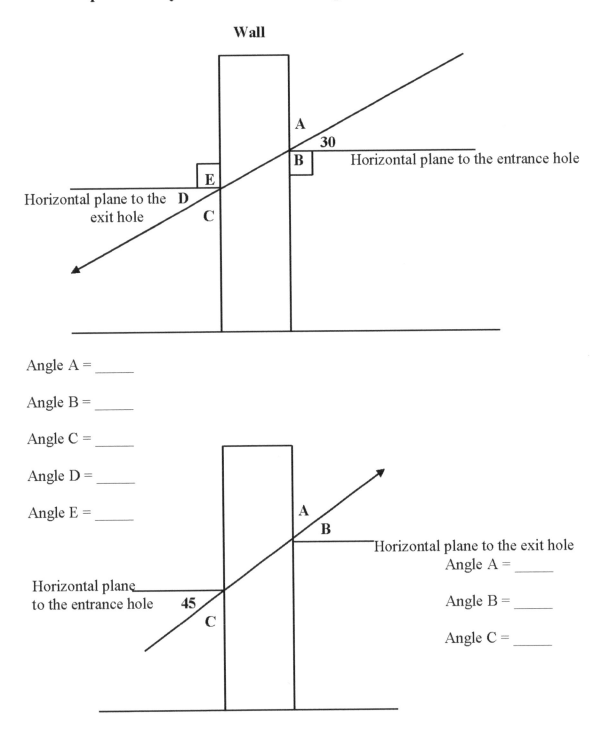

Angle A = _____

Angle B = _____

Angle C = _____

Angle D = _____

Angle E = _____

Angle A = _____

Angle B = _____

Angle C = _____

Math Review continued

Parallel lines intersected by a straight line

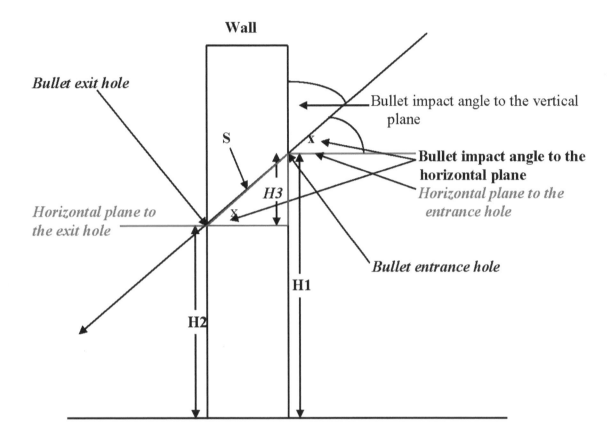

Wall

Bullet exit hole

Bullet impact angle to the vertical plane

S

Bullet impact angle to the horizontal plane
Horizontal plane to the entrance hole

Horizontal plane to the exit hole

H3

x

x

Bullet entrance hole

H1

H2

H1 represents the height of the bullet entrance hole
H2 represents the height of the bullet exit hole
H3 represents the difference in heights between the entrance and exit holes **H1** and **H2**
S represents the distance the bullet traveled through the wall

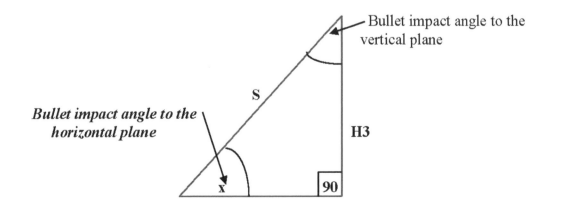

Bullet impact angle to the vertical plane

S

Bullet impact angle to the horizontal plane

H3

x

90

Math Review continued

Parallel lines intersected by a straight line

Practice Problems:

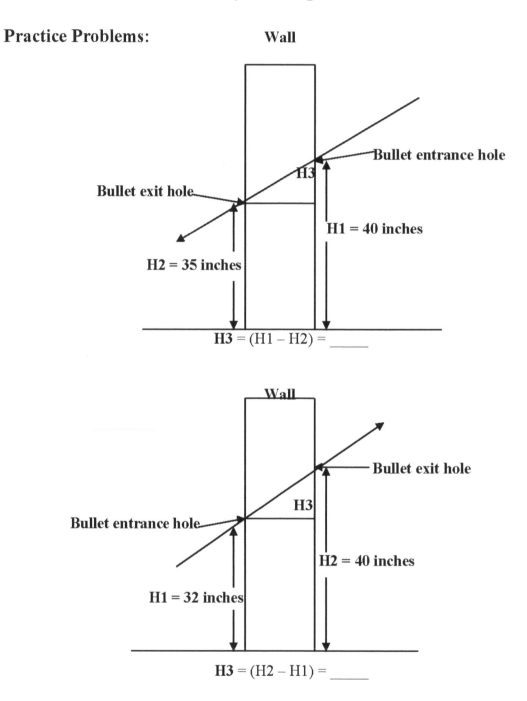

Wall

Bullet entrance hole

Bullet exit hole

H3

H1 = 40 inches

H2 = 35 inches

H3 = (H1 – H2) = _____

Wall

Bullet exit hole

Bullet entrance hole

H3

H2 = 40 inches

H1 = 32 inches

H3 = (H2 – H1) = _____

Math Review continued

Triangles

Definition: *Geometrical figure having three sides and three angles*

Any three-sided or three cornered figure, area or object, etc.

Any triangle may have two or more equal sides

(The *amount* of equal angles depend on the *number* of equal sides, that is, two equal sides – two equal angles and three equal sides – three equal angles)

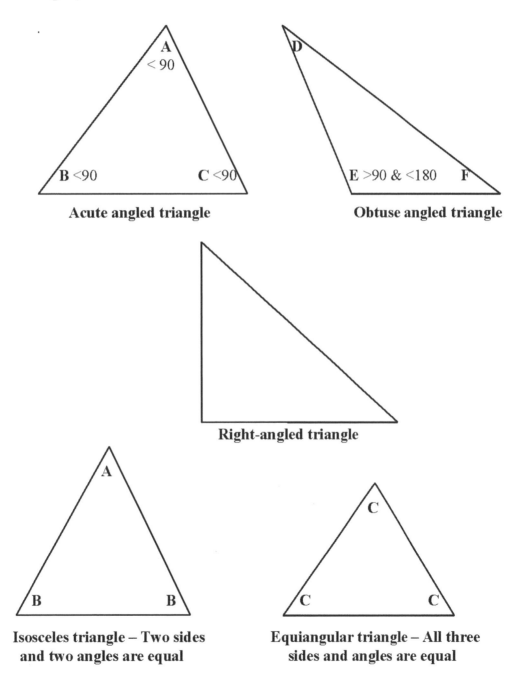

Acute angled triangle

Obtuse angled triangle

Right-angled triangle

Isosceles triangle – Two sides and two angles are equal

Equiangular triangle – All three sides and angles are equal

Math Review continued

Triangles

The sum of the angles of a triangle is always = 180 degrees

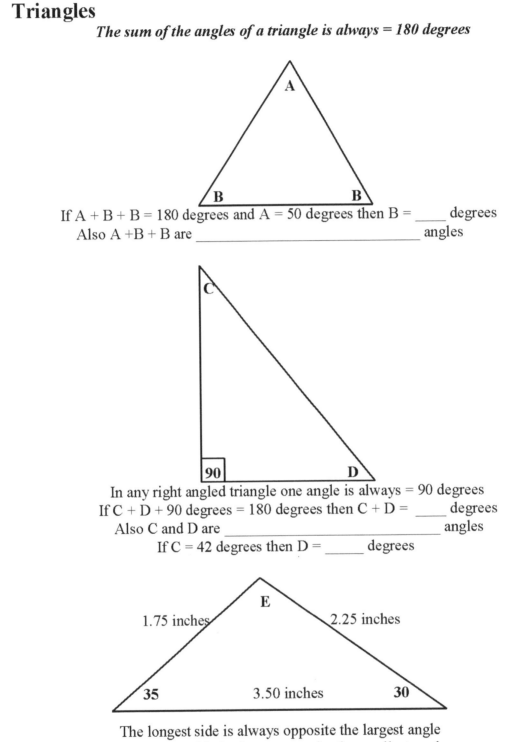

If A + B + B = 180 degrees and A = 50 degrees then B = _____ degrees

Also A +B + B are _____ angles

In any right angled triangle one angle is always = 90 degrees

If C + D + 90 degrees = 180 degrees then C + D = _____ degrees

Also C and D are _____ angles

If C = 42 degrees then D = _____ degrees

The longest side is always opposite the largest angle

The shortest side is always opposite the smallest angle

Angle E = _____ degrees

Math Review continued

Triangles
Practice Problems:

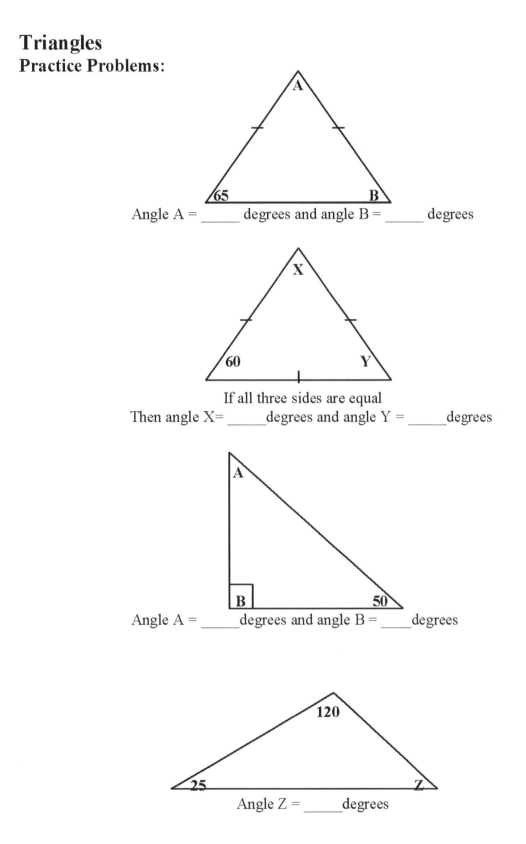

Angle A = _____ degrees and angle B = _____ degrees

If all three sides are equal
Then angle X= _____ degrees and angle Y = _____ degrees

Angle A = _____ degrees and angle B = _____ degrees

Angle Z = _____ degrees

Math Review continued

Right-angled Triangles:

One angle is always a right angle (90 degrees)
The other angles are complimentary (Their sum total 90 degrees)
The sides are named based on the angle in question

<u>Names:</u>

Adjacent side (adj.) – *The side next to or adjacent to angle in question* (angle A)
Opposite side (opp.) – *The side opposite the angle in question* (angle A)
Hypotenuse (hyp.) – *The side opposite the right angle* (The 90 degree angle)

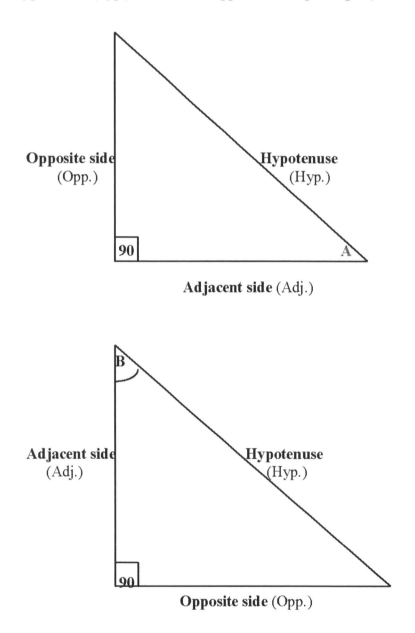

Opposite side (Opp.)

Hypotenuse (Hyp.)

90

A

Adjacent side (Adj.)

B

Adjacent side (Adj.)

Hypotenuse (Hyp.)

90

Opposite side (Opp.)

Math Review continued

Right-angled Triangles

Pythagorean theory

The square of the hypotenuse = The sum of the squares of the other sides

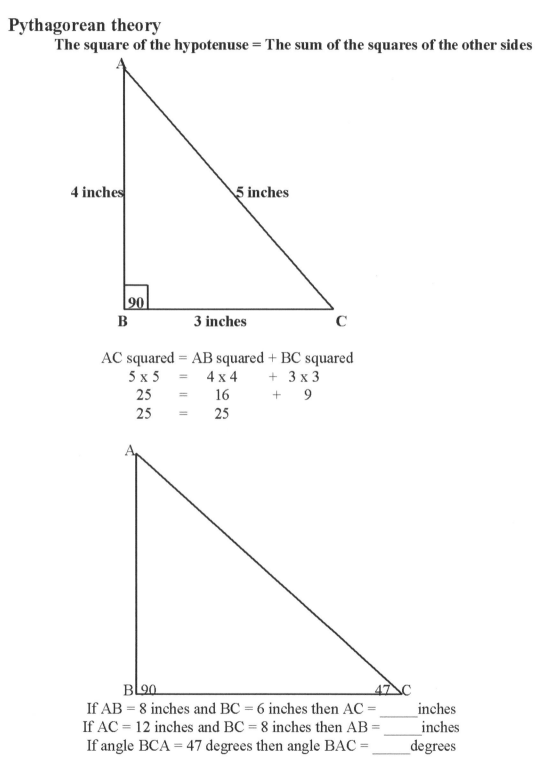

AC squared = AB squared + BC squared

5 x 5	=	4 x 4	+	3 x 3
25	=	16	+	9
25	=	25		

If AB = 8 inches and BC = 6 inches then AC = _____ inches

If AC = 12 inches and BC = 8 inches then AB = _____ inches

If angle BCA = 47 degrees then angle BAC = _____ degrees

Math Review continued

Right-angled triangles

Practice Problems

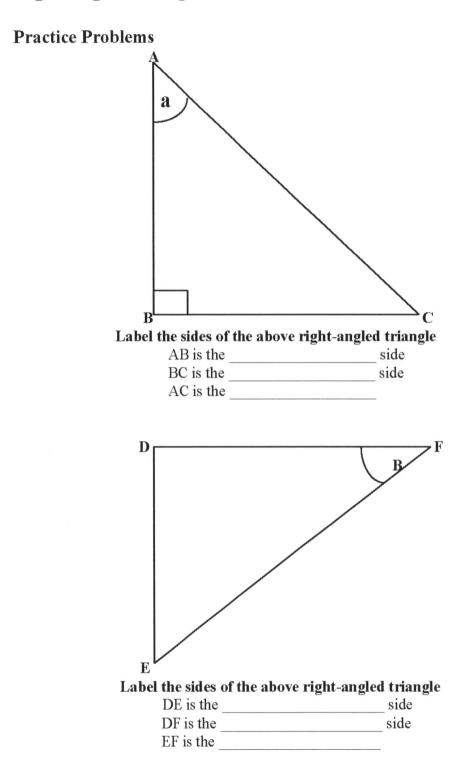

Label the sides of the above right-angled triangle

AB is the _____ side

BC is the _____ side

AC is the _____

Label the sides of the above right-angled triangle

DE is the _____ side

DF is the _____ side

EF is the _____

Math Review continued

Right-angle Triangles

Trigonometric Ratios

Sine abbreviated as **sin**   **= The length of the opposite side divided by the length of the hypotenuse**

Cosine abbreviated as **cos.**   **= The length of the adjacent side divided by the length of the hypotenuse**

Tangent abbreviated as **tan** **= The length of the opposite side divided by the length of the adjacent side**

```
                  a
                  /|
                 / |
  4 inches (adj. side)  5 inches (hypotenuse)
               /   |
              /    |
             /_____|
                  b
        3 inches (opp. side)
```

Sin **a** = The length of the opposite side
      the length of the hypotenuse

    = 3 inches
      5 inches

    = 0.6

   a = arc sin of 0.6

     = **36.9 or 37 degrees** *(To the nearest whole number)*

Cos **a** = The length of the adjacent side
      the length of the hypotenuse

    = 4 inches
      5 inches

    = 0.8

   a = arc cos 0.8

     = **36.9 or 37 degrees** *(To the nearest whole number)*

Tan **a** = The length of the opposite side
      the length of the adjacent side

    = 3 inches
      4 inches

    = 0.75

   a = arc tan 0.75

     = **36.9 or 37 degrees** *(To the nearest whole number)*

Making what you want to find *(the unknown) the subject* of the equation

A.   <u>Example:</u> **If the sin a = The opposite side / the hypotenuse and what you would like to find is the opposite side**

<u>*Solution:*</u>
*1.0 Since there is **an equal sign** in the above example then it is an equation so it is mathematically correct to **cross multiply***
If 3 = 6 / 2 then 6 = 2 x 3
*Thus **the opposite side = the hypotenuse x the sin of a***

*2.0 Also since the above example is **an equation** then it is mathematically correct to multiply both sides of the equation by **the same number***
If 3 = 6 / 2 then 3 x 2 = 6 / 2 x 2 or 3 x 2 = 6 (When simplified)
*Thus **sin of a x hypotenuse = the opposite side / the hypotenuse x hypotenuse** (Multiplying both sides of the equation by the hypotenuse)*
*Or **the opposite side = the hypotenuse x the sin of a** (The hypotenuses cancel out each other)*

B.   <u>Example:</u> **If the sine a = The opposite side / the hypotenuse and what you would like to find is the hypotenuse**

<u>*Solution:*</u>
This has to be done in two (2) stages
<u>**Step #1**</u> *(repeat of example A)*
   *1a. Since there is **an equal sign** in the above example then it is **an equation** so it is mathematically correct to **cross multiply***
   Again if 3 = 6 / 2 then 6 = 2 x 3
   *Thus **the opposite side = The hypotenuse x the sin of a***

   *1b. Also since the above example is **an equation** then it is mathematically correct to multiply both sides of the equation by **the same number***
   If 3 = 6 / 2 then 3 x 2 = 6 / 2 x 2 or 3 x 2 = 6 (When simplified)
   *Thus **sin a x the hypotenuse = the opposite side / the hypotenuse x the hypotenuse** (Multiplying both sides of the equation by the hypotenuse)*
   *Or **the opposite side = the hypotenuse x the sin of a** (The hypotenuses cancel out each other)*

<u>**Step #2**</u>
   2.0 Divide each side of the equation by 3
   6 / 3 = 3 x 2 / 3 or 2 = 6 / 3 (when simplified)
   Divide each side of the equation (step 1) by sin a
   *Thus **sin of a x the hypotenuse / the sin of a = The opposite side / the sin of a***
   *Or **the hypotenuse = the opposite side / the sin of a** (the two **sines** cancel out each other)*

Math Review continued

Right-angled Triangles

Practice Problems

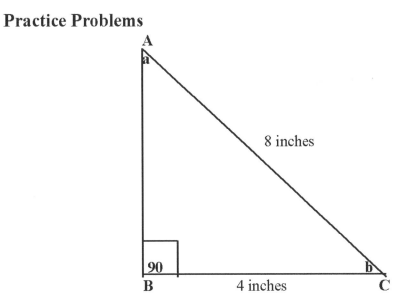

Calculate the other side and angles of the above triangle

Side AB = _____ inches
Angle a = _____ degrees
Angle b = _____ degrees

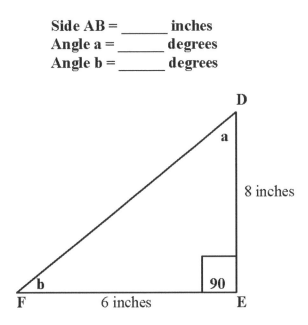

Calculate the other side and angles of the above triangle

Side DF = _____ inches
Angle a = _____ degrees
Angle b = _____ degrees

Math Review continued

Right-angled Triangles

Practice Problems

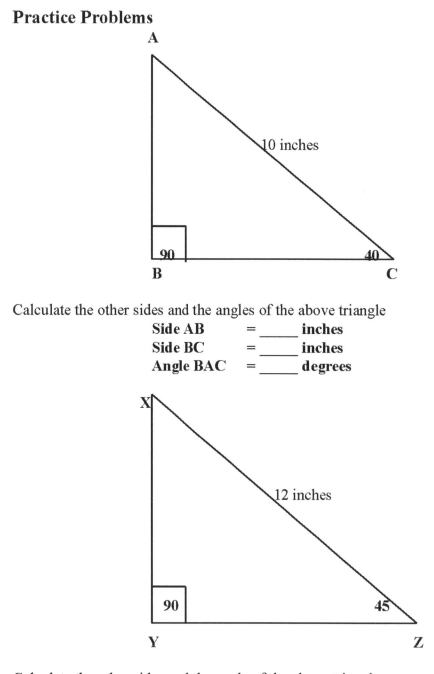

Calculate the other sides and the angles of the above triangle

                Side AB   = _____ **inches**

                Side BC   = _____ **inches**

                Angle BAC   = _____ **degrees**

Calculate the other sides and the angle of the above triangle

                Angle YXZ = _____ **degrees**

                Side XY   = _____ **inches**

                Side YZ   = _____ **inches**

Math Review continued

Right-angled Triangles

Practice Problems

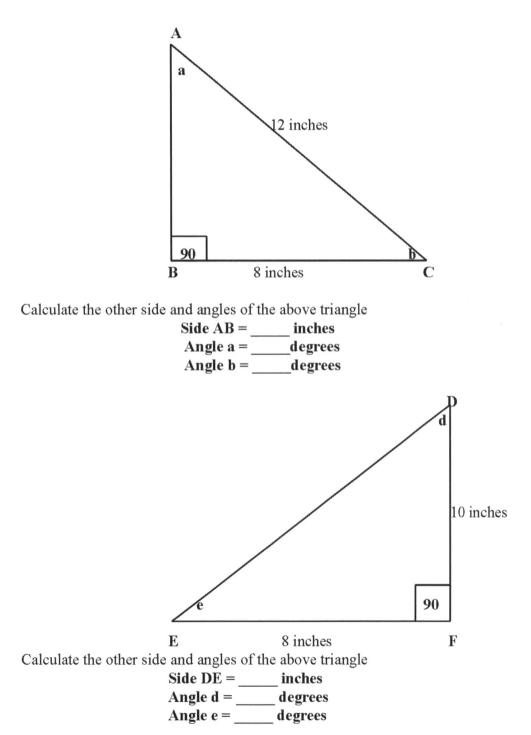

Calculate the other side and angles of the above triangle

> **Side AB =** _____ **inches**
> **Angle a =** _____ **degrees**
> **Angle b =** _____ **degrees**

Calculate the other side and angles of the above triangle

> **Side DE =** _____ **inches**
> **Angle d =** _____ **degrees**
> **Angle e =** _____ **degrees**

3A7. Determining the bullet entrance impact angles

Calculations
The information obtained for the scaled drawings will be the same for the calculations

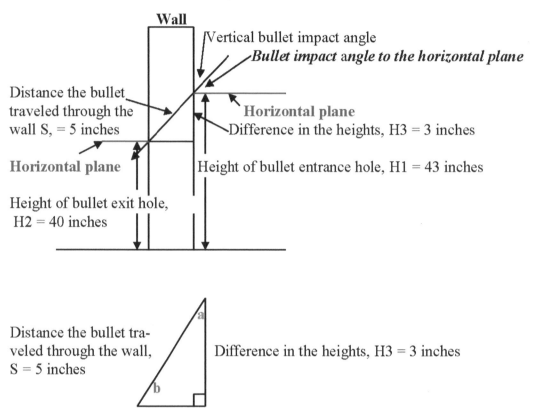

Examples:

1.0 <u>Vertical bullet impact angle</u> *(Not necessary for any reconstruction - Just for the math practice)*

- Height of the bullet entrance hole, H1	= 43 inches
- Height of the bullet exit hole, H2	= 40 inches
- Difference in these heights, H3	= (43 – 40) inches – 3 inches
- Distance the bullet traveled through the wall, S	= 5 inches

Formula:

Cosine *of a (abbreviated **cos.** of a)*	= The adjacent side (adj.) / the hypotenuse (hyp.)
	= The difference in the heights / the distance traveled
Therefore the vertical bullet impact angle, a	= H3 divided by S
	= 3 inches / 5 inches
	= 0.6
	= arc cosine of 0.6
	= 53 degrees

3A7. Determining the bullet entrance impact angles

Calculations continued

2.0 Bullet impact angle to the horizontal plane *(Required for any reconstruction)*
- Height of the bullet entrance hole, H1   = 43 inches
- Height of the bullet exit hole, H2   = 40 inches
- Difference in these heights, H3   = 3 inches
- Distance the bullet traveled through the wall, S = 5 inches

Formula:

        Sine *of* **b** *(abbreviated as* **sin** *of* **b**)   = The opposite side (opp.) /
                                           the hypotenuse (hyp.)
                                        = The difference in the heights
                                        / the distance traveled

Therefore the bullet impact angle to the horizontal plane, b = H3 divided by S
                                                   = 3 inches / 5 inches
                                                   = 0.6
                                                   = arc sine of 0.6
                                                 = **37 degrees**

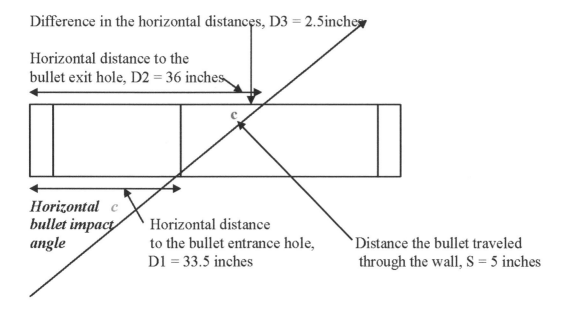

Difference in the horizontal distances, D3 = 2.5inches

Horizontal distance to the
bullet exit hole, D2 = 36 inches

c

Horizontal c
bullet impact
angle   Horizontal distance
                     to the bullet entrance hole,   Distance the bullet traveled
                     D1 = 33.5 inches   through the wall, S = 5 inches

3A7. Determining the bullet entrance impact angles

Calculations continued

3.0 Horizontal bullet impact angle *(Required for a shooting reconstruction)*

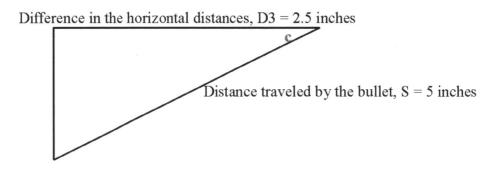

Difference in the horizontal distances, D3 = 2.5 inches

Distance traveled by the bullet, S = 5 inches

- Horizontal distance to the bullet entrance hole, D1	= 33.5 inches
- Horizontal distance to the bullet exit hole, D2	= 36 inches
- Difference in the horizontal distances, D3	= 2.5 inches
- Distance the bullet traveled through the wall, S	= 5 inches

Formula:

    Cosine *of c (abbreviated as **cos.** c)*   = The adjacent side (adj.) / the hypotenuse (hyp.)
    = The difference in the horizontal distances / the distance traveled through the wall

Therefore the horizontal bullet impact angle, c = D3 divided by S
= (36 –33.5) inches / 5 inches
= 2.5 inches / 5 inches
= 0.5
= arc cos. of 0.5
= **60 degrees**

3A7. Determining the bullet entrance impact angles

Calculations for bullet hole #1

The dimensions that were used for the scaled drawings would also be used for the following calculations _(page 18)_

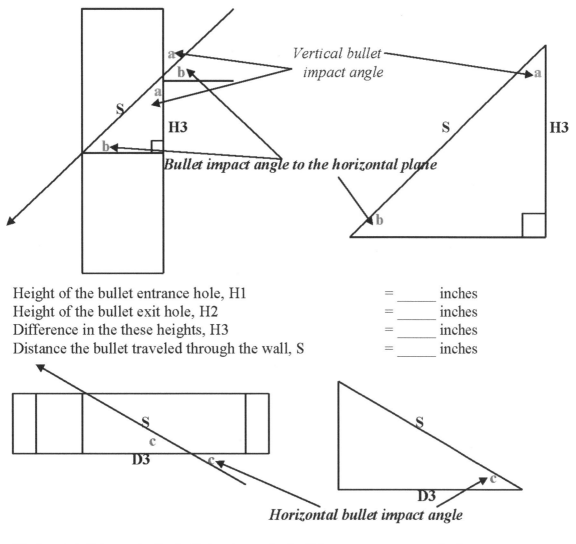

Height of the bullet entrance hole, H1	= _____	inches
Height of the bullet exit hole, H2	= _____	inches
Difference in the these heights, H3	= _____	inches
Distance the bullet traveled through the wall, S	= _____	inches

Horizontal distance to the bullet entrance hole, D1	= _____	inches
Horizontal distance to the bullet exit hole, D2	= _____	inches
Difference in these horizontal distances, D3	= _____	inches
Distance the bullet traveled through the wall, S	= _____	inches

3A7.   Determining the bullet entrance impact angles

Do your calculations for bullet hole #1 below *(Enter your results for #2 and #3 in the tables on pages 71 to 73)*

1.0 Vertical bullet impact angle, a *(Not necessary for any reconstruction – Just for the math practice)*

2.0 Bullet impact angle to the horizontal plane, b

3.0 Horizontal bullet impact angle, c

3A7. Determining the bullet entrance impact angles

Calculations for bullet hole #2

The dimensions that were used for the scaled drawings would also be used for the following calculations *(page 18)*

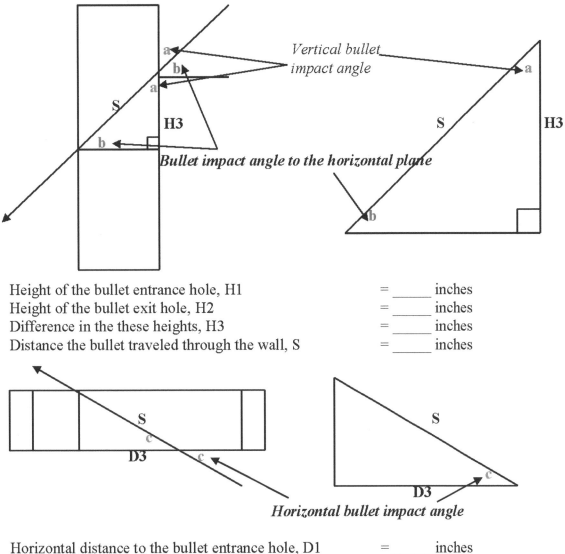

Height of the bullet entrance hole, H1   = _____ inches
Height of the bullet exit hole, H2   = _____ inches
Difference in the these heights, H3   = _____ inches
Distance the bullet traveled through the wall, S   = _____ inches

Horizontal distance to the bullet entrance hole, D1   = _____ inches
Horizontal distance to the bullet exit hole, D2   = _____ inches
Difference in these horizontal distances, D3   = _____ inches
Distance the bullet traveled through the wall, S   = _____ inches

3A7.   Determining the bullet entrance impact angles

Do your calculations for bullet hole #2 below (*Enter your results for #2 and #3 in the tables on pages 71 to 73*)

1.0 <u>Vertical bullet impact angle</u>, a *(Not necessary for any reconstruction - Just for the math practice)*

2.0 <u>Bullet impact angle to the horizontal plane</u>, b

3.0 <u>Horizontal bullet impact angle</u>, c

3A7. Determining the bullet entrance impact angles

Calculations for bullet hole #3

The dimensions that were used for the scaled drawings would also be used for the following calculations _(page 18)_

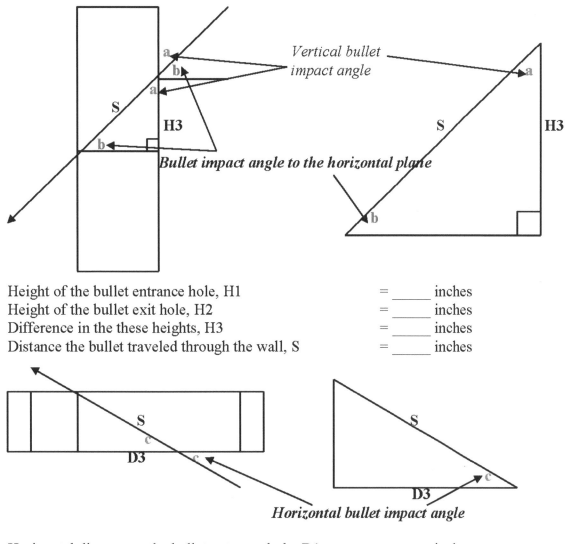

Height of the bullet entrance hole, H1   = _____ inches
Height of the bullet exit hole, H2   = _____ inches
Difference in the these heights, H3   = _____ inches
Distance the bullet traveled through the wall, S   = _____ inches

Horizontal distance to the bullet entrance hole, D1   = _____ inches
Horizontal distance to the bullet exit hole, D2   = _____ inches
Difference in these horizontal distances, D3   = _____ inches
Distance the bullet traveled through the wall, S   = _____ inches

3A7.   Determining the bullet entrance impact angles

Do your calculations for bullet hole #3 below *(Enter your results for #2 and #3 in the tables on pages 71 to 73)*

1.0 <u>Vertical bullet impact angle,</u> a *(Not necessary for any reconstruction – Just for the math practice)*

2.0 <u>Bullet impact angle to the horizontal plane,</u> b

3.0 <u>Horizontal bullet impact angle,</u> c

Comparison of the bullet impact entrance angles

Note: *The bullet entrance impact angles to the horizontal plane would always be necessary to reconstruct the shooting incident. Thus this angle should always be determined at least three different ways and then the mean or average angle used in the determination of the location of the muzzle of the weapon.*

If one uses the shape of the bullet entrance hole or a protractor to find the bullet entrance impact angle to the surface one could still determine the angle to the horizontal plane by subtracting that angle from 90 degrees.

Comparison & average or mean of the impact entrance angles

Bullet impact entrance angles to the horizontal plane *(Angles measured vertically - Up or down)*

Bullet hole #1	Measuring devices	Bullet impact entrance angles to the horizontal plane
	Protractor	
	Smart level Smart laser	
	Laser trac	
	Angle finder	
	Scaled drawings	
	Calculations	
	Sum of the bullet impact entrance angles to the horizontal plane	
	Average or mean of the bullet impact entrance angles to the horizontal plane	

Horizontal bullet impact entrance angles *(Angles measured horizontally)*

Bullet hole #1	Measuring devices	Horizontal bullet impact entrance angles
	Protractor	
	Scaled drawings	
	Calculations	
	Sum of the horizontal bullet impact entrance angles	
	Average or mean of the horizontal bullet impact entrance angles	

Comparison of the bullet impact entrance angles

Note: *The bullet entrance impact angles to the horizontal plane would always be necessary to reconstruct the shooting incident. Thus this angle should always be determined at least three different ways and then the mean or average angle used in the determination of the location of the muzzle of the weapon.*

If one uses the shape of the entrance hole or a protractor to find the bullet entrance impact angle to the surface one could still determine the angle to the horizontal plane by subtracting that angle from 90 degrees.

Comparison & average or mean of the impact entrance angles

Bullet impact entrance angles to the horizontal plane *(Angles measured vertically – Up or down)*

Bullet hole #2	Measuring devices	Bullet impact entrance angles to the horizontal plane
	Protractor	
	Smart level Smart laser	
	Laser trac	
	Angle finder	
	Scaled drawings	
	Calculations	
	Sum of the bullet impact entrance angles to the horizontal plane	
	Average or mean of the bullet impact entrance angles to the horizontal plane	

Horizontal bullet impact entrance angles *(Angles measured horizontally)*

Bullet hole #2	Measuring devices	Horizontal bullet impact entrance angles
	Protractor	
	Scaled drawings	
	Calculations	
	Sum of the horizontal bullet impact entrance angles	
	Average or mean of the horizontal impact entrance angles	

Comparison of the bullet impact entrance angles

Note: *The entrance bullet impact angles to the horizontal plane would always be necessary to reconstruct the shooting incident. Thus this angle should always be determined at least three different ways and then the mean or average angle used in the determination of the location of the muzzle of the weapon.*

If one uses the shape of the entrance hole or a protractor to find the bullet entrance impact angle to the surface one could still determine the angle to the horizontal plane by subtracting that angle from 90 degrees.

Comparison & average or mean of the impact entrance angles

Bullet impact entrance angles to the horizontal plane *(Angles measured vertically – Up or down)*

Bullet hole #3	Measuring devices	Bullet impact entrance angles to the horizontal plane
	Protractor	
	Smart level Smart laser	
	Laser trac	
	Angle finder	
	Scaled drawings	
	Calculations	
	Sum of the bullet impact entrance angles to the horizontal plane	
	Average or mean of the bullet impact entrance angles to the horizontal plane	

Horizontal bullet impact entrance angles *(Angles measured horizontally)*

Bullet hole #3	Measuring devices	Horizontal bullet impact entrance angles
	Protractor	
	Scaled drawings	
	Calculations	
	Sum of the horizontal bullet impact entrance angles	
	Average or mean of the horizontal bullet impact entrance angles	

Calculating *the percentage error* for the different methods used to determine the two (2) bullet entrance impact angles

Comparison of the different methods used for each type of impact angle

1.0 Bullet impact entrance angles to the horizontal plane

Methods	Angles of bullet hole #1 for each method	% error from the mean or average for each method	Angles of bullet hole #2 for each method	% error from the mean or average for each method	Angles of bullet hole #3 for each method	% error from the mean or average for each method
Protractor						
Smart level Smart laser						
Laser trac						
Angle finder						
Scaled drawings						
Calculations						
Sum of the angles for each hole						
Mean or average of the angles for each hole						

2.0 Horizontal bullet impact entrance angles

Methods	Angles of bullet hole #1 for each method	% error from the mean or average for each hole	Angles of bullet hole #2 for each method	% error from the mean or average for each hole	Angles of bullet hole #3 for each method	% error from the mean or average for each hole
Protractor						
Scaled drawings						
Calculations						
Sum of the angles for each hole						
Mean or average of the angles for each hole						

Assignment #4 – Determining *the bullet entrance impact angle* from an extended dowel rod

Calculating the bullet entrance impacts angles from an extended dowel rod

Training objectives
At the conclusion of the segment, the student should be able to:

A. Determine the bullet impact entrance angle to the horizontal plane with the use of a protruding dowel rod from the bullet impact entrance hole and the corresponding second impact bullet hole or site of the wall

B. Determine the horizontal bullet impact entrance angle to a vertical surface with the use of a protruding dowel rod from the bullet impact entrance hole and the corresponding second impact bullet hole or site of the wall

1.0 Bullet impact entrance angle to the horizontal plane

1.0 Check the surface *(table)* below the path of the extended dowel rod to ascertain that it is level

2.0 Mark two (2) spots on the dowel rod about twelve inches apart

3.0 Measure the distance between those two marked spots

4.0 Measure the height of each marked spot above the surface *(table)*

5.0 Determine the difference in heights of the two marked spots

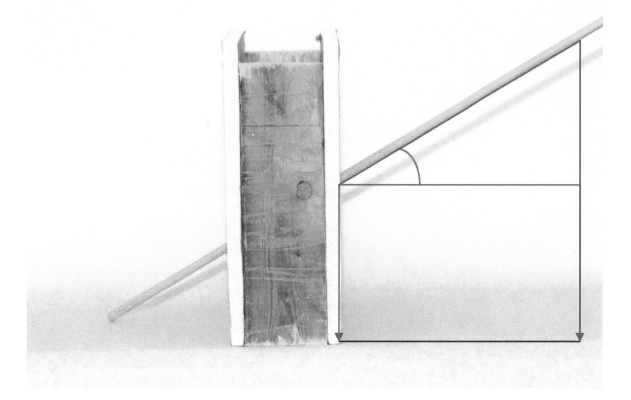

The bullet impact entrance angle to the horizontal plane could then be determined from the blue-lined triangle with the use of the sine *(sin)* ratio.

Formula:
> **Sin** of the angle = The opposite side / the hypotenuse
> > = The difference in heights / the distance between the two marks on the dowel rod

2.0   Horizontal bullet entrance impact angle
1.0   Mark two (2) spots on the dowel rod about twelve inches apart
2.0   Measure the distance between those two marked spots
3.0   Measure the horizontal perpendicular distance from each marked spot to the surface of the wall
4.0   Determine the difference in the horizontal distances of the two marked spots

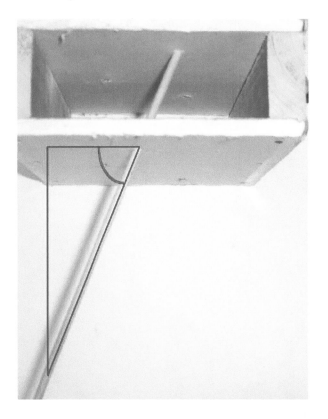

The horizontal bullet impact entrance angle to the right when facing the wall could then be determined from the blue-lined triangle with the use of the sine *(sin)* ratio.

Formula:
> Sin of the angle = The opposite side / the hypotenuse
> > = The difference in the horizontal distances / the distance between the two marks on the dowel rod

Information to determine your bullet impact entrance angles by *calculation*

Bullet Hole #1
Bullet impact entrance angle to the horizontal plane
Height of the higher mark on the dowel rod =

Height of the lower mark on the dowel rod =

Differences in these two heights =

Distance between the two marks on the dowel rod =

Horizontal bullet impact entrance angle
Horizontal distance of the mark that is further away from the wall =

Horizontal distance of the mark that is closer to the wall =

Differences in these two horizontal distances =

Distance between the two marks on the dowel rod =

Information to determine your bullet impact entrance angles by *calculation*

Bullet Hole #2

Bullet impact entrance angle to the horizontal plane

Height of the higher mark on the dowel rod   =

Height of the lower mark on the dowel rod   =

Differences in these two heights   =

Distance between the two marks on the dowel rod   =

Horizontal bullet impact entrance angle

Horizontal distance of the mark that is further away from the wall   =

Horizontal distance of the mark that is closer to the wall   =

Differences in these two horizontal distances   =

Distance between the two marks on the dowel rod   =

Information to determine your bullet impact entrance angles by
calculation

Bullet Hole #3
Bullet impact entrance angle to the horizontal plane

Height of the higher mark on the dowel rod   =
Height of the lower mark on the dowel rod   =
Differences in these two heights   =
Distance between the two marks on the dowel rod   =

Horizontal bullet impact entrance angle

Horizontal distance of the mark that is further away from the wall =
Horizontal distance of the mark that is closer to the wall   =
Differences in these two horizontal distances   =
Distance between the two marks on the dowel rod   =

Assignment #5 –Determining *the bullet impact entrance angles* in the driver's door of a truck *(or any vehicle)*

Training objectives

At the conclusion of the segment, the student should be able to:

A.   Determine the bullet impact entrance angle to the horizontal plane of a curved or non-plumb surface with the use of a protruding dowel rod from the bullet impact entrance hole and the corresponding second impact bullet hole or site

B.   Determine the horizontal bullet impact entrance angle to a curved or non- plumb surface with the use of a protruding dowel rod from the bullet impact entrance hole and the corresponding second impact bullet hole or site

1.0   Bullet impact entrance angle to the horizontal plane

a.   Check the surface below the path of the extended dowel rod to ascertain that it is level

b.   Mark two (2) spots on the dowel rod about twelve inches apart

c.   Measure the distance between those two marked spots on the dowel rod

d.   Measure the height of each marked spot on the dowel rod above the ground

e.   Determine the difference in heights of the two marked spots on the dowel rod

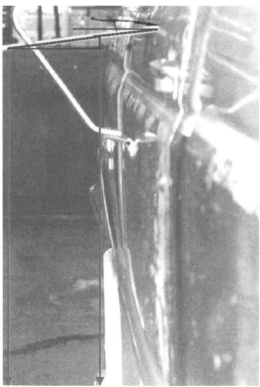

The bullet impact entrance angle to the horizontal plane could be calculated from the right angled triangle in red at the base of the dowel rod
(Vertically opposite angles)

Bullet impact entrance angle to the horizontal plane

Information needed to calculate the bullet impact entrance angle to the horizontal plane

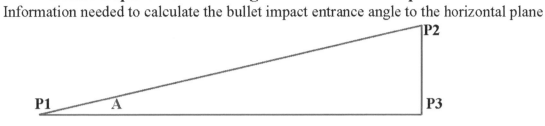

Example:

Distance between the marks on the dowel rod (P1 to P2)	= 12.0 inches
Height of mark, P2	= 46.0 inches
Height of mark, P1	= 44.5 inches
Difference in the heights of P2 and P1	= 1.5 inches
Bullet impact entrance angle to the horizontal plane A	= ?

Formula to solve for A *(The bullet impact entrance angle to the horizontal plane)*

Sin of A
$$= \text{The opposite side / the hypotenuse}$$
$$= \text{The difference in the heights / the distance from P1 to P2}$$
$$= 1.5 \text{ inches} / 12.0 \text{ inches}$$
$$= 0.125$$
$$= \text{arc sin } 0.125$$
= 7.2 degrees

The above information could be also used to determine the slope of a windshield or the hood

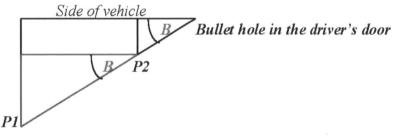

Information to determine the horizontal bullet impact entrance angle

Distance between the marks on the dowel (P1 to P2)	= 12.0 inches
Horizontal distance from mark, P2	= 2.0 inches
Horizontal distance from mark, P1	= 11.0 inches
Difference in the horizontal distances	= 9.0 inches
Horizontal impact entrance angle B	= ?

Formula to solve for B *(The horizontal bullet impact entrance angle)*

Sin of B
$$= \text{The opposite side / the hypotenuse}$$
$$= \text{The difference in the horizontal distances / the distance from } \mathbf{P1} \text{ to } \mathbf{P2}$$
$$= 9.0 \text{ inches} / 12.0 \text{ inches}$$
$$= 0.75$$
$$= \text{arc sin } 0.75$$
= 48.6 degrees

Training Objectives

At the conclusion of this training segment, the student should be able to:

    A. Determine the horizontal distances from the muzzle of a gun to the bullet impact site for any given muzzle height using the methods listed below

    B. Determine the distances traveled from the muzzle of a gun to the bullet impact site for any given muzzle height using the methods listed below

Determining the location of the muzzle of the gun

<u>Note:</u> The documentation of the bullet hole(s) and the determination of the bullet impact entrance angles should always be done before attempting to establish the possible locations of the victim and or shooter.

Also the ***most likely*** locations of the muzzle of the gun and subsequently the possible locations of the shooter at the time of the incident may be determined by using one or more of the following methods:

1.0 String(s)

2.0 Scaled Drawing(s)

3.0 Calculation(s)

*The height of the entrance hole **must** be taken into consideration:*

*a.   **Downward bullet impact entrance angles to the horizontal plane** – The height of the bullet entrance hole must be subtracted from the height of the muzzle of the gun when determining the horizontal distance and the distance traveled by scaled drawings and or calculations.*

*b.   **Upward bullet impact entrance angles to the horizontal plane** – The height of the muzzle of the gun must be subtracted from the height of the bullet entrance hole when determining the horizontal distance and the distance traveled by scaled drawings and or calculations.*

Also the information obtained from the strings and scaled drawings methods could be verified by calculations.

Determining *the location of the muzzle of a gun*

A. Downward or sloped bullet impact entrance angles to the horizontal plane

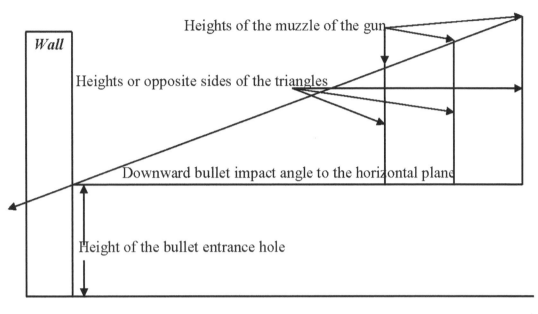

Floor

Note: *The height of the bullet impact entrance site (bullet hole or indentation) does not have to be known when using the string method to determine the horizontal distances or the distances traveled but is necessary to complete the right angles triangles for the scaled drawings and calculations.*

B. Upward or inclined bullet impact entrance angles to the horizontal plane

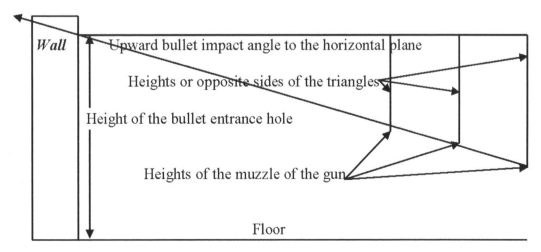

Floor

Assignment #6 - Determining *the horizontal distances* and *the distances traveled* from the muzzle of a gun to the bullet impact site *(bullet entrance hole or indentation)* using the *string method*

Bullet entrance and corresponding exit holes for #1

Place the best fitting dowel rod through bullet entrance hole #1 and the corresponding bullet exit hole then attach a string to the exposed section of the dowel rod on the entrance side of the wall

Secure the dowel rod on the exit side of the wall to prevent it from being pulled through the wall

Extend the string parallel to the dowel rod and attach the other end to a fixed location

Place an extended rule on the floor with the ***zero-end*** against the wall directly below the section of the dowel rod with the attached string

Measure the horizontal distances and the distances traveled *(along the string)* for the corresponding heights of 12, 24, 36, 48, 60, 72 and 84 inches or 12, 18, 24, 30, 36, 42 and 48 inches *if your bullet impact entrance angle to the horizontal plane is small*

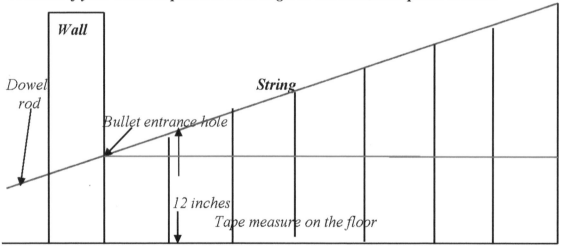

Note: *The bullet impact entrance angle to the horizontal plane is not necessary for the* ***string method***

Muzzle heights in inches	Horizontal distances **in inches**	Distances traveled **in inches**

Assignment #6 - Determining *the horizontal distances* and *the distances traveled* from the muzzle of a gun to the bullet impact site *(bullet entrance hole or indentation)* using the <u>*string method*</u>

Bullet entrance and corresponding exit holes for #2

Place the best fitting dowel rod through bullet entrance hole #2 and the corresponding bullet exit hole then attach a string to the exposed section of the rod on the entrance side of the wall

Secure the dowel rod on the exit side of the wall to prevent it from being pulled through the wall

Extend the string parallel to the dowel rod and attach the other end to a fixed object or location

Place an extended rule on the floor with the <u>*zero-end*</u> against the wall directly below the section of the dowel rod with the attached string

Measure the horizontal distances and the distances traveled *(along the string)* for the corresponding heights of 12, 24, 36, 48, 60, 72 and 84 inches or 12, 18, 24, 30, 36, 42 and 48 inches *if your bullet impact entrance angle to the horizontal plane is small*

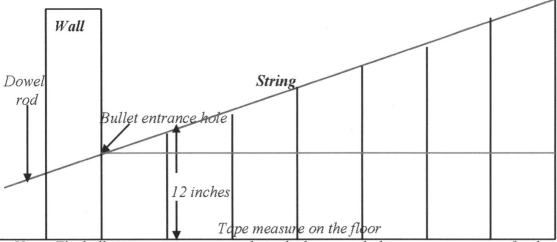

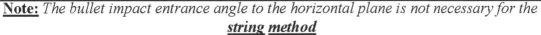

Note: *The bullet impact entrance angle to the horizontal plane is not necessary for the* <u>*string method*</u>

Muzzle heights in inches	Horizontal distances in inches	Distances traveled in inches

Assignment #6 - Determining *the horizontal distances* and *the distances traveled* from the muzzle of a gun to the bullet impact site *(bullet entrance hole or indentation)* using the *string method*

Bullet entrance and corresponding exit holes for #3

Place the best fitting dowel rod through bullet entrance hole #3 and the corresponding bullet exit hole then attach a string to the exposed section of the rod on the entrance side of the wall

Secure the dowel rod on the exit side of the wall to prevent it from being pulled through the wall

Extend the string parallel to the dowel rod and attach the other end to a fixed object or location

Place an extended rule on the floor with the *zero-end* against the wall directly below the section of the dowel rod with the attached string

Measure the horizontal distances and the distances traveled *(along the string)* for the corresponding heights of 12, 24, 36, 48, 60, 72 and 84 inches or 12, 18, 24, 30, 36, 42 and 48 inches *if your bullet impact entrance angle to the horizontal plane is small*

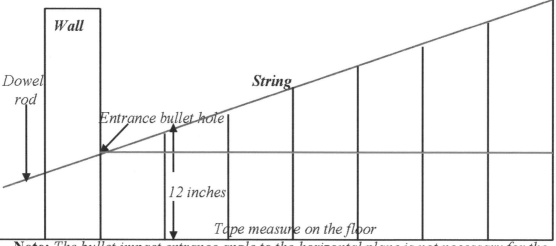

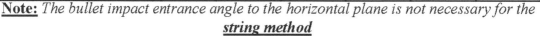

Note: *The bullet impact entrance angle to the horizontal plane is not necessary for the* ___string method___

Muzzle heights in inches	Horizontal distances *in inches*	Distances traveled *in inches*

Assignment #7 - Determining *the horizontal distances* and *the distances traveled* from the muzzle of a gun to the bullet impact site *(bullet entrance hole or indentation)* using the *scaled drawing* method

Bullet entrance and corresponding exit holes for #1

Note: *The bullet impact entrance angle to the horizontal plane is required to complete the right angled triangle for the scaled drawing method*

Subtract the height of the bullet entrance hole from the 12 inch height and each other height
- *This distance would represent the opposite side of your right angled triangle ABC*
- *Determine the best scale to be to use to maximize your scaled drawings on your paper*

Draw line BC to represent the opposite side of the right angled triangle ABC
From C draw line AC to make angle C or ABC complimentary of angle A or ABC
From B draw line BA perpendicular to BC to intersect line AC
Complete the triangles for the other differences in the heights

Measure the base *(the horizontal distances)* **and the hypotenuses** *(The distances traveled)* **of each right angled triangle and multiply those distances by your scale**

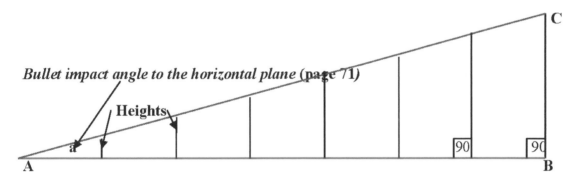

Muzzle heights in inches	Horizontal distances *in inches*	Distances traveled *in inches*

Assignment #7 continued

Complete your scaled drawing(s) for bullet entrance hole #1 below

Assignment #7 - Determining *the horizontal distances* and *the distances traveled* from the muzzle of a gun to the bullet impact site *(bullet entrance hole or indentation)* using the <u>scaled drawing</u> method

Bullet entrance and corresponding exit holes for #2

<u>Note:</u> *The bullet impact entrance angle to the horizontal plane is required to complete the right angled triangle for the scaled drawing method*

Subtract the height of the bullet impact entrance hole from the 12 inch height and each other height
- *This distance would represent the opposite side of your right angled triangle ABC*
- *Determine the best scale to be to use to maximize your scaled drawings on your paper*

Draw line BC to represent the opposite side of the right angled triangle ABC
From C draw line AC to make angle C or ABC complimentary of angle A or ABC
From B draw line BA perpendicular to BC to intersect line AC
Complete the triangles for the other differences in the heights

Measure the base *(the horizontal distances)* and the hypotenuses *(The distances traveled)* of each right angled triangle and multiply those distances by your scale

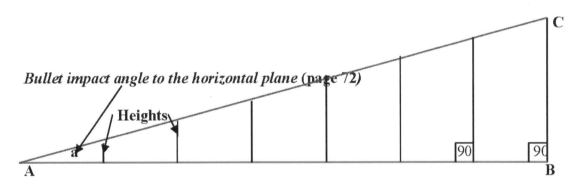

Muzzle heights in inches	Horizontal distances in inches	Distances traveled in inches

Assignment #7 continued

Complete your scaled drawing(s) for bullet entrance hole #2 below

Assignment #7 - Determining *the horizontal distances* and *the distances traveled* from the muzzle of a gun to the bullet impact site *(bullet entrance hole or indentation)* using the <u>*scaled drawing*</u> method

Bullet entrance and corresponding exit holes for #3

<u>Note:</u> *The bullet impact entrance angle to the horizontal plane is required to complete the right angled triangle for the scaled drawing method*

Subtract the height of the bullet entrance hole from the 12 inch height and each other height
- *This distance would represent the opposite side of your right angled triangle ABC*
- *Determine the best scale to be to use to maximize your scaled drawings on your paper*

Draw line BC to represent the opposite side of the right angled triangle ABC
From C draw line AC to make angle C or ABC complimentary of angle A or ABC
From B draw line BA perpendicular to BC to intersect line AC
Complete the triangles for the other differences in the heights

Measure the base *(the horizontal distances)* and the hypotenuses *(The distances traveled)* of each right angled triangle and multiply those distances by your scale

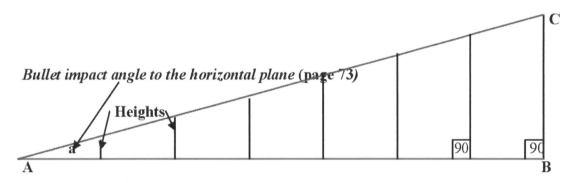

Muzzle heights in inches	Horizontal distances in inches	Distances traveled in inches

Assignment #7 continued

Complete your scaled drawing(s) for bullet entrance hole #3 below

Assignment #8 - Determining *the horizontal distances* and *the distances traveled* from the muzzle of a gun to the bullet impact site *(bullet entrance hole or indentation)* using the *calculations* method

Note: The bullet impact entrance angle to the horizontal plane is required to calculate the base *(the horizontal distance)* and the hypotenuse *(The distance traveled)* of your right angled triangle

The horizontal distances and the distances traveled from the muzzle of the gun could be calculated using the following trigonometric ratios

Note: *The height of the bullet entrance hole **must** be subtracted from the height of the muzzle of the gun to the calculate the horizontal distances and the distances traveled*

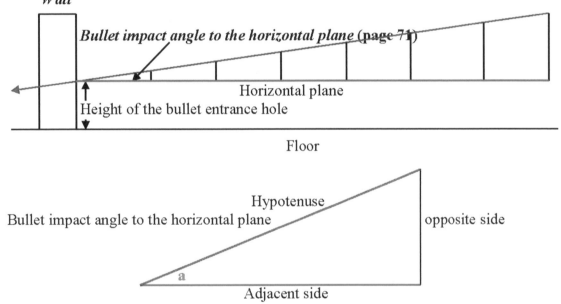

Formula to find the horizontal distance (the adjacent side) from the opposite side *(the difference in the heights)* and the bullet impact angle *(the bullet impact entrance angle to the horizontal plane)*

Tangent (abbreviated as **tan**) of a = The opposite side / the adjacent side
Or the opposite side = The adjacent side x the tan of a
Or the adjacent side = The opposite side / the tan of a
Therefore the horizontal distance of the muzzle of the gun
= *The opposite side / the tan of a*

93

Example:

Information to calculate the horizontal distance to the muzzle of the gun

Bullet impact entrance angle to the horizontal plane	= 25 degrees
Height of the bullet entrance hole	= 7.5 inches
Height of the muzzle of the gun	= 12 inches
Difference in the heights for the 1st triangle	= 4.5 inches
Horizontal distance for the 12 inch height	= 4.5 inches / tan 25 degrees
	= 4.5 inches / 0.466
	= **9.65 inches**

Information to calculate the horizontal distances from the muzzle of the gun for the other muzzle heights (opposite sides)

Bullet impact entrance angle to the horizontal plane	= 25 degrees
Difference in the heights for the 2nd triangle (Opposite side)	= Muzzle height - 7.5 inches
Horizontal distance for the 2nd muzzle height	= Opp. side / tan 25 degrees
Difference in the heights for the 3rd triangle (Opposite side)	= Muzzle height - 7.5 inches
Horizontal distance for the 3rd muzzle height	= Opp. side / tan 25 degrees

Same for the other muzzle heights

Formula to find the distance traveled *(the hypotenuse)* **from the opposite side** *(the difference in the heights)* **and the bullet impact angle** *(the bullet entrance impact angle to the horizontal plane)*

Sine (abbreviated as **sin**) of a	= Opposite side / hypotenuse
Or the opposite side	= Hypotenuse x the sin of a
Or the hypotenuse	= Opposite side / the sin of a
Therefore the distance traveled from the muzzle of the gun	
	= *Opposite side / the sin of a*

Example:

Information to calculate the distance traveled from the muzzle of the gun

Bullet impact entrance angle to the horizontal plane	= 25 degrees
Height of the bullet entrance hole	= 7.5 inches
Difference in the heights for the 1st triangle	= 4.5 inches
Therefore the opposite side	= 4.5 inches
Distance traveled for the 12 inch height	= 4.5 inches / sin 25 degrees
	= 4.5 inches / 0.423
	= **10.64 inches**

Information to calculate the distances traveled from the muzzle of the gun for the other muzzle heights (opposite sides)

Bullet impact entrance angle to the horizontal plane	= 25 degrees
Difference in the heights for the 2nd triangle (Opposite side)	= Muzzle height - 7.5 inches
Distance traveled for the 2nd muzzle height	= Opp. side / sin25 degrees
Difference in the heights for the 3rd triangle (Opposite side)	= Muzzle height - 7.5 inches
Distance traveled for the 3rd muzzle height	= Opp. side / sin 25 degrees

Same for the other muzzle heights

Assignment #8 continued

Calculations for bullet entrance hole #1

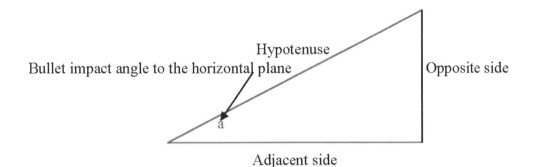

Hypotenuse

Bullet impact angle to the horizontal plane

Opposite side

a

Adjacent side

Information to calculate the horizontal distance from the muzzle of the gun to surface with the bullet hole or indentation

Bullet impact entrance angle to the horizontal plane   = _____ degrees
Height of the bullet entrance hole   = _____ inches
Height of the muzzle of the gun   = _____ inches
Difference in the heights for the 1st triangle *(Opposite side)* = _____ inches

Formula to calculate the horizontal distance

Tangent (abbreviated as **tan**) of **a**   = Opposite side / the adjacent side
Or the opposite side   = Adjacent side x the tan of **a**
Or the adjacent side   = Opposite side / the tan of **a**
Therefore the horizontal distance of the muzzle of the gun
      = ***The opposite side / the tan of a***

Information to calculate the distance traveled from the muzzle of the gun to the bullet impact site (bullet hole or indentation)

Bullet impact entrance angle to the horizontal plane   = _____ degrees
Height of the bullet entrance hole   = _____ inches
Height of the muzzle of the gun   = _____ inches
Difference in the heights for the 1st triangle *(Opposite side)* = _____ inches

Formula to calculate the horizontal distance

Sine (abbreviated as **sin**) of **a**   = Opposite side / the hypotenuse
Or the opposite side   = Hypotenuse x the tan of **a**
Or the hypotenuse   = Opposite side / the sin of **a**
Therefore the distance traveled from the muzzle of the gun to the impact site (bullet hole or indentation)
      = ***The opposite side / the sin of a***

Assignment #8 continued

Do your calculations for bullet entrance hole #1 below

Assignment #8 continued

Calculations for bullet entrance hole #2

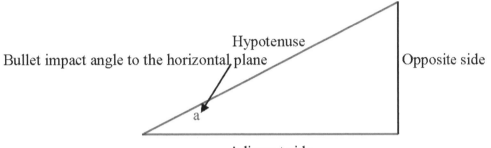

Information to calculate the horizontal distance from the muzzle of the gun to surface with the hole or indentation

Bullet impact entrance angle to the horizontal plane = _____ degrees
Height of the bullet entrance hole = _____ inches
Height of the muzzle of the gun = _____ inches
Difference in the heights for the 1st triangle *(Opposite side)* = _____ inches

Formula to calculate the horizontal distance

Tangent (abbreviated as **tan**) of **a** = Opposite side / the adjacent side
Or the opposite side = Adjacent side x the tan of **a**
Or the adjacent side = Opposite side / the tan of **a**
Therefore the horizontal distance of the muzzle of the gun
= The opposite side / the tan of a

Information to calculate the distance traveled from the muzzle of the gun to the bullet impact site (bullet hole or indentation)

Bullet impact entrance angle to the horizontal plane = _____ degrees
Height of the bullet entrance hole = _____ inches
Height of the muzzle of the gun = _____ inches
Difference in the heights for the 1st triangle *(Opposite side)* = _____ inches

Formula to calculate the horizontal distance

Sine (abbreviated as **sin**) of **a** = The opposite side / the hypotenuse
Or the opposite side = The hypotenuse x the tan of **a**
Or the hypotenuse = The opposite side / the sin of **a**
Therefore the distance traveled from the muzzle of the gun to the impact site (bullet hole or indentation)
= The opposite side / the sin of a

Assignment #8 continued

Do your calculations for bullet entrance hole #2 below

Assignment #8 continued

Calculations for bullet entrance hole #3

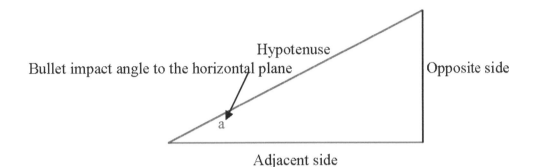

Hypotenuse

Bullet impact angle to the horizontal plane

Opposite side

a

Adjacent side

Information to calculate the horizontal distance from the muzzle of the gun to surface with the hole or indentation

Bullet impact entrance angle to the horizontal plane   = ____ degrees
Height of the bullet entrance hole   = ____ inches
Height of the muzzle of the gun   = ____ inches
Difference in the heights for the 1st triangle *(Opposite side)* = ____ inches

Formula to calculate the horizontal distance

Tangent (abbreviated as **tan**) of **a**   = Opposite side / the adjacent side
Or the opposite side   = Adjacent side x the tan of **a**
Or the adjacent side   = Opposite side / the tan of **a**
Therefore the horizontal distance of the muzzle of the gun

     = ***The opposite side / the tan of a***

Information to calculate the distance traveled from the muzzle of the gun to the bullet impact site *(bullet hole or indentation)*

Bullet impact entrance angle to the horizontal plane   = ____ degrees
Height of the bullet entrance hole   = ____ inches
Height of the muzzle of the gun   = ____ inches
Difference in the heights for the 1st triangle *(Opposite side)* = ____ inches

Formula to calculate the horizontal distance

Sine (abbreviated as **sin**) of **a**   = Opposite side / the hypotenuse
Or the opposite side   = Hypotenuse x the tan of **a**
Or the hypotenuse   = Opposite side / the sin of **a**
Therefore the distance traveled from the muzzle of the gun to the impact site (bullet hole or indentation)

     = ***The opposite side / the sin of a***

Assignment #8 continued

Do your calculations for bullet entrance hole #3 below

Comparison of the locations of the muzzle of the gun

The horizontal distances from the muzzle of the gun to the surface with the bullet hole and the distances traveled by the bullet from the muzzle of the gun to the impact site could be compared for each muzzle height.

- *The string method and or photographs of the string(s) in place would serve as a very good visual aid for anyone associated with the reconstruction.*
The string method should be the least accurate because of all of the problems such as finding a place and the method of how to anchor the string, the tension of the string, the length and weight of the string that would cause it to sag and the ability to correctly measure the necessary distances.

- *The scaled drawing method would also provide a visual representation for anyone associate with the reconstruction.*
The scaled drawing is time consuming and the accuracy of the drawing will depend on the equipment and the skills of the individual doing the drawing.

- *The calculation method would be much faster and more accurate but an understanding and a working knowledge of the trigonometric ratios would be necessary perform the reconstruction.*
The calculations can be done at the scene in a very short time if one has a scientific calculator and or the trigonometric tables

Horizontal distances (*Adjacent sides of the right angled triangles*) for bullet hole #1

Methods	1st height	2nd height	3rd height	4th height	5th height	6th height	7th height
String							
Scaled drawing							
Calculation							

Distances traveled (*Hypotenuses of the right angled triangles*) for bullet hole #1

Methods	1st height	2nd height	3rd height	4th height	5th height	6th height	7th height
String							
Scaled drawing							
Calculation							

Horizontal distances *(Adjacent sides of the right angled triangles)* **for bullet hole #2**

Methods	1st height	2nd height	3rd height	4th height	5th height	6th height	7th height
String							
Scaled drawing							
Calculation							

Distances traveled *(Hypotenuses of the right angled triangles)* **for bullet hole #2**

Methods	1st height	2nd height	3rd height	4th height	5th height	6th height	7th height
String							
Scaled drawing							
Calculation							

Horizontal distances *(Adjacent sides of the right angled triangles)* **for bullet hole # 3**

Methods	1st height	2nd height	3rd height	4th height	5th height	6th height	7th height
String							
Scaled drawing							
Calculation							

Distances traveled *(Hypotenuses of the right angled triangles)* **for bullet hole #3**

Methods	1st height	2nd height	3rd height	4th height	5th height	6th height	7th height
String							
Scaled drawing							
Calculation							

Assignment #9 – Determining *the horizontal distances* and *the distances traveled* using <u>scaled drawings</u> method for the muzzle heights of 48, 54 and 60 inches

Training Objectives

At the conclusion of this training segment, the student should be able to:

A.   Determine the horizontal distances from the muzzle of a gun to the wall with the bullet impact entrance hole for any given muzzle height

B.   Determine the distances traveled from the muzzle of a gun to the bullet impact entrance hole in the wall for any given muzzle height

Note: *The <u>most</u> <u>likely</u> locations of the muzzle of the gun and subsequently the possible locations of the shooter at the time of the incident may be determined by using one or more of the following methods:*

1.0 Scaled Drawing(s)

2.0 String(s)

3.0 Calculation(s)

Determining *the horizontal distances* from the muzzle of the gun and the *distances traveled* from the muzzle to the bullet hole in the wall at the muzzle heights of 48, 54 and 60 inches using <u>scaled drawings</u>

Information needed for drawing the diagram to determine the horizontal distance from the muzzle of the gun to the wall
Example:

-	Heights of the muzzle of the gun	= 48, 54 and 60 inches
-	Height of the bullet entrance hole	= 33 inches
-	Difference in the heights	= 15, 21 and 27 inches
-	Bullet impact angle to the horizontal plane	= 15 degrees

Completing the triangle from the above information
     Note: *The best scale should be used to maximize the size of the diagram*

Instructions for drawing the right-angled triangle using your scale:
1.0   Draw line AB to represent the difference in the heights
2.0   From B draw line BC perpendicular (90 degrees) to line AB
3.0   From A make angle A or BAC equal to 75 degrees
4.0   Draw line AC to meet line BC
5.0   Measure line BC and multiply that distance by your scale to determine its actual distance *(the horizontal distance from muzzle to the wall with the bullet hole)*

6.0   Measure line AC and multiply that distance by your scale to determine its actual distance (*The distance traveled from the muzzle to the bullet hole in the wall*)

7.0   Complete the triangles for the two other muzzle heights *(54 & 60 inches)* and determine the actual horizontal distances and the distances traveled

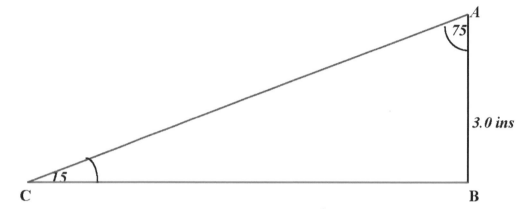

<u>Note:</u> *If the scale is "1 inch is approximately equal to 5 inches" then AB = 3.0 inches*

Draw the <u>*scaled drawings*</u> for the two other muzzle heights below

Assignment #10 - Determining *the horizontal distances* and *the distances traveled* using the *string* method for the muzzle heights of 48, 54 and 60 inches

Training Objectives

At the conclusion of this training segment, the student should be able to:

A. Determine the horizontal distances from the muzzle of a gun to the wall with the bullet hole for any given muzzle height

B. Determine the distances traveled from the muzzle of a gun to the bullet hole in the wall for any given muzzle height

Determine *the horizontal distances* traveled from the muzzle of the gun to the wall with the bullet hole and the *distances traveled* from the muzzle to the bullet hole at the muzzle heights of 48, 54 and 60 inches using the *string* method

NOTE: *Complete Assignment #14 before removing your string(s)*

Attach a string to a wall in your classroom at a height of 33 inches and attach the other end of the string to the adjacent perpendicular wall to make an upward angle of 15 degrees to the horizontal plane and a horizontal angle of 40 degrees with the extended string

Place an extended rule on the floor rule with the zero-end against the wall directly below the section of the dowel rod with the attached string

Determine the horizontal distances and the distances traveled from the muzzle of the gun to the bullet hole in the wall for the corresponding muzzle heights of 48, 54 and 60 inches

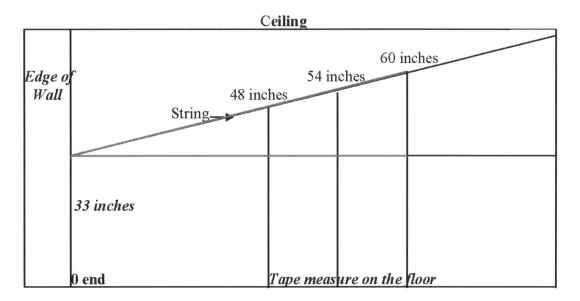

Draw your rough diagram(s) for the *string* method below

Assignment #11 - Determine *the horizontal distances* from the muzzle of the gun to the wall and *the distances traveled* from the muzzle to the bullet hole at the muzzle heights of 48, 54 and 60 inches by *calculations*

Example:

Note: The height of the bullet entrance hole ***must*** be subtracted from the height of the muzzle of the gun before doing the calculations

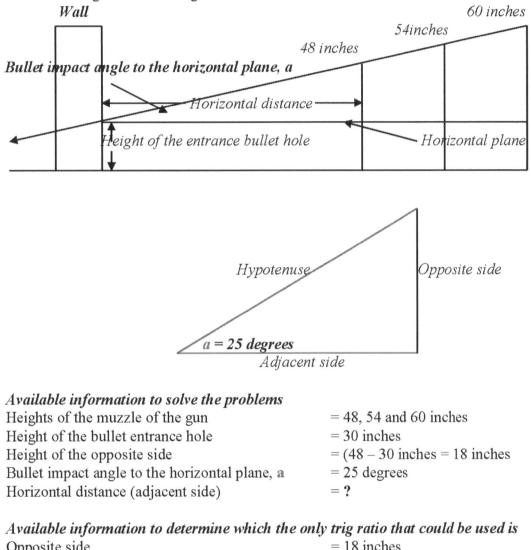

Available information to solve the problems

Heights of the muzzle of the gun	= 48, 54 and 60 inches
Height of the bullet entrance hole	= 30 inches
Height of the opposite side	= (48 – 30 inches = 18 inches
Bullet impact angle to the horizontal plane, **a**	= 25 degrees
Horizontal distance (adjacent side)	= ?

Available information to determine which the only trig ratio that could be used is

Opposite side	= 18 inches
Angle in question	= 25 degrees
Adjacent side	= ?

Based on the above information the ONLY formula that could be used is

Tangent (tan) of 25 degrees	= Opposite side / the adjacent side
Adjacent side x the tangent of 25 degrees	= The opposite side
Or the adjacent side	**= Opposite side / tan of 25 degrees**

Solving for the 48, 54 and 60 inches muzzle heights

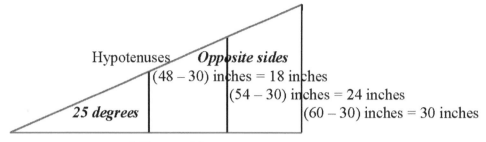

Hypotenuses / *Opposite sides*

(48 – 30) inches = 18 inches

(54 – 30) inches = 24 inches

25 degrees   (60 – 30) inches = 30 inches

Adjacent sides

Solving for the 48 inches muzzle height
Horizontal distance (adjacent side)   = Opposite side / tan of 25 degrees
= 18 inches / 0.467
= 38.5 inches

Solving for the 54 inches muzzle height
Horizontal distance (adjacent side)   = Opposite side / tan of 25 degrees
= 24 inches / 0.467
= 51.4 inches

Solving for the 60 inches muzzle height
Horizontal distance (adjacent side)   = Opposite side / tan of 25 degrees
= 30 inches / 0.467
= 64.2 inches

Available information to solve the problems
Heights of the muzzle of the gun   = 48, 54 and 60 inches
Height of the bullet entrance hole   = 30 inches
Height of the opposite side   = (48 – 30) inches = 18 inches
Bullet impact angle to the horizontal plane, a   = 25 degrees
Distance traveled (hypotenuse)   = ?

Available information to determine which the only trig ratio that could be used is
Opposite side   = 18inches
Angle in question   = 25 degrees
Hypotenuse   = ?

Based on the above information the <u>ONLY</u> formula that could be used is
Sine (sin) of 25 degrees   = Opposite side / the hypotenuse
Hypotenuse x the sin of 25 degrees   = Opposite side
Or the hypotenuse   **= Opposite side / sin of 25 degrees**

Solving for the 48 inches muzzle height
Distance traveled (hypotenuse)   = Opposite side / sin of 25 degrees
= 18 inches / 0.423
= 42.6 inches

Solving for the 54 inches muzzle height
Horizontal distance (adjacent side) = Opposite side / sin of 25 degrees
= 24 inches / 0.423
= 56.7 inches

Solving for the 60 inches muzzle height
Horizontal distance (adjacent side) = Opposite side / sin of 25 degrees
= 30 inches / 0.423
= 70.9 inches

<u>Calculate</u> your distances from the information in assignment #9 below

Comparison of the locations of the muzzle of the gun

Compare *the horizontal distances* from the muzzle of the gun to the wall
for the three holes *(Assignments #9 through #11)*

Bullet hole #1

Heights of the muzzle	Horizontal Distances (*string*)	Horizontal Distances (*scaled drawings*)	Horizontal Distances (*calculations*)	Total of the Horizontal Distances	Average or Mean	% Error from the Av. or Mean
48 ins						
54 ins						
60 ins						

Bullet hole #2

Heights of the muzzle	Horizontal distances (*string*)	Horizontal distances (*scaled drawings*)	Horizontal distances (*calculations*)	Total of the Horizontal Distances	Average or Mean	% Error from the Av. or Mean
48 ins						
54 ins						
60 ins						

Bullet hole #3

Heights of the muzzle	Horizontal distances (*string*)	Horizontal distances (*scaled drawings*)	Horizontal distances (*calculations*)	Total of the Horizontal Distances	Average or Mean	% Error from the Av. or Mean
48 ins						
54 ins						
60 ins						

Comparison of the locations of the muzzle of the gun

Compare *the distances traveled* from the muzzle of the gun to the three holes in the wall *(Assignments #9 through #11)*

Bullet hole #1

Heights of the muzzle	Distances Traveled *(string)*	Distances Traveled *(scaled drawings)*	Distances Traveled *(calculations)*	Total of the Distances Traveled	Average or Mean	% Error from the Av. or Mean
48 ins						
54 ins						
60 ins						

Bullet hole #2

Heights of the muzzle	Distances traveled *(string)*	Distances Traveled *(scaled drawings)*	Distances Traveled *(calculations)*	Total of the Distances Traveled	Average or Mean	% Error from the Av. or Mean
48 ins						
54 ins						
60 ins						

Bullet hole #3

Heights of the muzzle	Distances Traveled *(string)*	Distances Traveled *(scaled drawings)*	Distances Traveled *(calculations)*	Total of the Distances Traveled	Average or Mean	% Error from the Av. or Mean
48 ins						
54 ins						
60 ins						

Assignment #12 – Determining *the perpendicular horizontal distances* using <u>*scaled drawings*</u>

Training Objectives

At the conclusion of this training segment, the student should be able to:

A.   Determine the horizontal *perpendicular* distances from the muzzle of the gun to the wall with the bullet impact entrance hole for the muzzle of heights of 48, 54 and 60 inches

B.   Determine the distances along the wall from the bullet impact entrance hole to where the *perpendicular* lines for the same muzzle heights of 48, 54 and 60 inches would meet the wall

<u>Note:</u> *The <u>most</u> <u>likely</u> horizontal perpendicular locations of the muzzle of the gun and subsequently the possible locations of the shooter at the time of the incident may be determined by using one or more of the following methods:*

1.0   **Scaled Drawing(s)**

2.0   **String(s)**

3.0   **Calculation(s)**

Determining *the horizontal perpendicular distances* from the muzzle of the gun to the wall with the bullet hole(s) and *the distances* from the bullet entrance hole in the wall to the location where the perpendicular lines will meet the wall with the bullet hole(s) for the muzzle heights of 48, 54 and 60 inches using a <u>*scaled drawing*</u>

Information needed for drawing the diagram to determine the horizontal <u>perpendicular</u> distances from the muzzle of the gun to the wall

Example:
-     Horizontal distances for the muzzle heights of   48, 54 and 60 inches
-     Horizontal bullet impact entrance angle   **= 40 degrees**

Completing the triangle from the above information
        <u>*Note: The best scale should be used to maximize the size of the diagram*</u>

Instructions for drawing the right-angled triangle:
1.0   Draw line AB to represent the wall with the bullet impact entrance hole
2.0   From A draw line AC *(red line)* at 40 degrees to line AB
3.0   From B draw line BC perpendicular to AB to complete the large triangle ABC

4.0   From A use your scale to mark the horizontal distances on line AC *(red line)* for the three muzzle heights of 48, 54 and 60 inches

5.0   From these three marks on line AC draw three *green lines* perpendicular to line AB *(the wall)*

6.0   Measure the lengths of those three lines and multiply by your scale to obtain the actual perpendicular distances

7.0   Measure the distances along line AB *(blue line)* to the three *green lines* and multiply those distances by your scale to obtain the actual distances along the wall

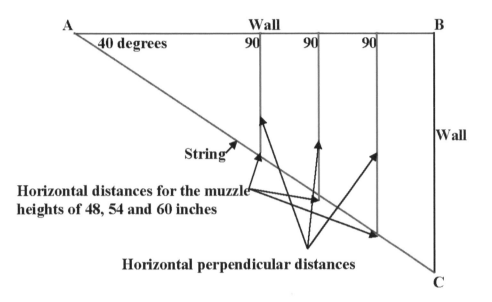

Draw your <u>scaled diagram</u> for this assignment below

Assignment # 13 – Determining *the perpendicular horizontal distances* using _strings_

Training Objectives

At the conclusion of this training segment, the student should be able to:

A.   Determine the horizontal *perpendicular* distances from the muzzle of the gun to the wall with bullet impact entrance hole for the muzzle of heights of 48, 54 and 60 inches using the *string* method

B.   Determine the distances along the wall from the bullet impact entrance hole to where the perpendicular lines for the same muzzle heights of 48, 54 and 60 inches would meet the wall using the *string* method

Determining *the perpendicular horizontal distances (green lines)* from the muzzle of the gun to the wall with the bullet hole(s) and the *distances (blue lines)* from the bullet entrance hole in the wall to the location where the perpendicular lines will meet the wall with the bullet hole for the muzzle heights of 48, 54 and 60 inches using the _string_ method

Classroom walls

-   Attach a string to a wall in your classroom at a height of 33 inches and attach the other end of the string to the adjacent perpendicular wall to make a horizontal angle of 40 degrees with the extended string

-   Place an extended rule with the zero-end against the wall on the floor directly below the extended string

-   Determine the perpendicular horizontal distances to the wall with the impact site and the horizontal distance along the wall for each muzzle height 48, 54 and 60 Inches

Side view of the string
Ceiling

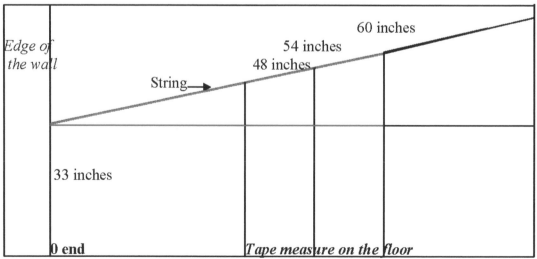

114

Top view of the wall

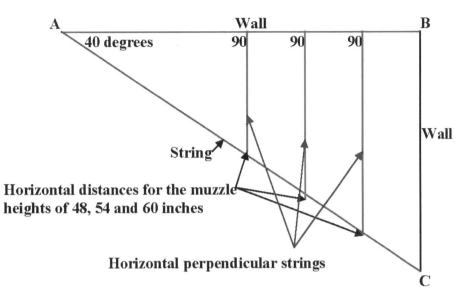

Draw your rough sketches for your <u>string</u> method below

Assignment # 14 - Determining *the perpendicular horizontal distances* using *calculations*

Training Objectives

At the conclusion of this training segment, the student should be able to:

A.   Determine the *perpendicular* horizontal distances from the muzzle of the gun to the bullet impact site for the muzzle of heights of 48, 54 and 60 inches by calculations

B.   Determine the *distances* along the wall from the bullet impact site to where the perpendicular lines for the same muzzle heights of 48, 54 and 60 inches intersect the wall by calculations

Determining *the perpendicular horizontal distances* (*green lines*) from the muzzle of the gun to the wall with the bullet hole(s) and the *distances* (*blue lines*) from the bullet impact sites in the wall to the location where the perpendicular lines will meet the wall with the bullet hole(s) for muzzle heights of 48, 54 and 60 inches by *calculations*

Available information to solve the problem

Note: *These distances were calculated for the 25 degree angle to the horizontal plane and muzzle heights of 48, 54 and 60 inches in assignment #12*
Horizontal distance *(now the hypotenuse)* for 48 inches muzzle height   **= 38.6 inches**
Horizontal distance *(now the hypotenuse)* for 54 inches muzzle height   **= 51.5 inches**
Horizontal distance *(now the hypotenuse)* for 60 inches muzzle height   **= 63.4 inches**
Horizontal angle   **= 40 degrees**

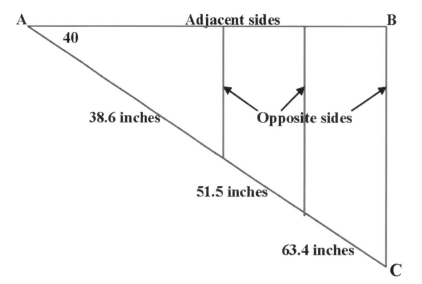

Available information to determine the _ONLY_ formula that could be used to calculate the perpendicular distance:

Hypotenuse = 38.6 inches
Angle in question = 40 degrees
Opposite side *(green lines)* = ?
Sine (sin) of 40 degrees = The opposite side / the hypotenuse
= The perpendicular horizontal distance / the horizontal distance
Perpendicular horizontal distance = The horizontal distance x the sin of 40 degrees

48 inches muzzle height
Perpendicular horizontal distance = 38.6 inches x 0.643
= 24.8 inches

54 inches muzzle height
Perpendicular horizontal distance = 51.5 inches x 0.643
= 33.1 inches

60 inches muzzle height
Perpendicular horizontal distance = 63.4 inches x 0.643
= 40.8 inches

Available information to determine the _ONLY_ formula that could be used to calculate the horizontal distance along the wall with the impact site:

Hypotenuse = 38.6 inches
Angle in question = 40 degrees
Adjacent side *(blue lines)* = ?

Cosine (cos) of 40 degrees = The adjacent side / the hypotenuse
= The distance along the wall the horizontal distance
Horizontal distance along the wall = The horizontal distance x the sin of 40 degrees

48 inches muzzle height
Horizontal distance along the wall = 38.6 inches x 0.766
= 29.6 inches

54 inches muzzle height
Horizontal distance along the wall = 51.5 inches x 0.766
= 39.4 inches

60 inches muzzle height
Horizontal distance along the wall = 63.4 inches x 0.766
= 48.6 inches

Assignment #14 continued

Calculate the perpendicular horizontal distances and *the horizontal distances* to the walls below

Comparison of the locations of the muzzle of the gun

Compare *the horizontal perpendicular distances* from the muzzle of the gun to the extended string / line at the front of the wall for the three holes *(Assignments #12 through #14)*

Heights of the muzzle	Horizontal Perpendicular Distances *(string)*	Horizontal Perpendicular Distances *(scaled drawings)*	Horizontal Perpendicular Distances *(calculations)*	Total of the Perpendicular Distances	Average or Mean	% Error from the Av. or Mean
48 ins						
54 ins						
60 ins						

Comparison of the locations of the muzzle of the gun

Compare *the horizontal distances* along the wall from the holes to the intersection of the corresponding perpendicular and extended string / line at the front of the wall for the three holes *(Assignments #12 through #14)*

Heights of the muzzle	Horizontal Distances *(string)*	Horizontal Distances *(scaled drawings)*	Horizontal distances *(calculations)*	Total of the Horizontal Distances	Average or Mean	% Error from the Av. or Mean
48 ins						
54 ins						
60 ins						

Assignment #15 – Classroom using strings

Classroom Assignment

Attach one end of a string about three (3) feet above the floor to a wall in the classroom

Stretch the string as much as possible and attach the other to the opposite wall about six to seven and a half *(6 – 7.5)* feet above the floor.

Measure the perpendicular distance between those two walls *(width of the room)*

Measure the height and horizontal distances of each end of the string where it is attached to the two walls

Wall *(lower end of string)*

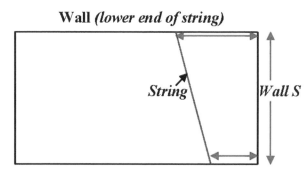

Opposite wall *(higher end of string)*
Floor plan of the room (view from above)

Ceiling

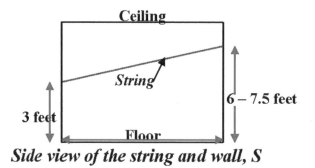

Side view of the string and wall, S

Information needed to solve the assignment:
- Height of the lower end of the string   = ____ inches
- Height of the higher end of the string   = ____ inches
- Horizontal distance from the lower end of the string to wall S   = ____ inches
- Horizontal distance from the higher end of the string to wall S = ____ inches
- Length (horizontal distance) of wall S   = ____ inches

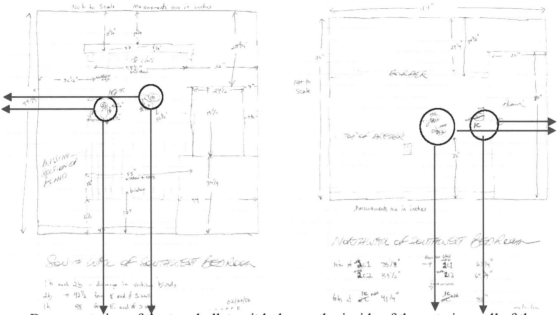

Documentation of the two bullet exit holes on the inside of the exterior wall of the
bedroom wall and the three bullet entrance holes in the opposite wall of the bedroom
One of the two bullets separated into two pieces after penetrating the exterior wall of the
bedroom *(That is the reason for the three bullet entrance holes in the opposite wall of the
bedroom of the house)*

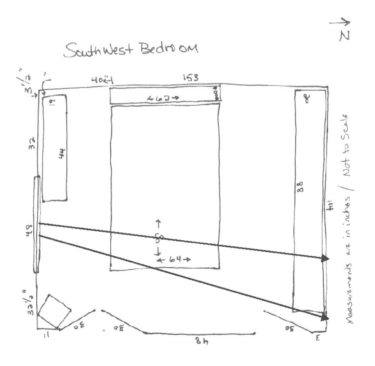

Documentation of the floor plan of the bedroom with the five bullet holes
*(The two blue arrows indicate the most likely path of the bullet and the
two bullet fragments that penetrated the opposite wall of the bedroom)*

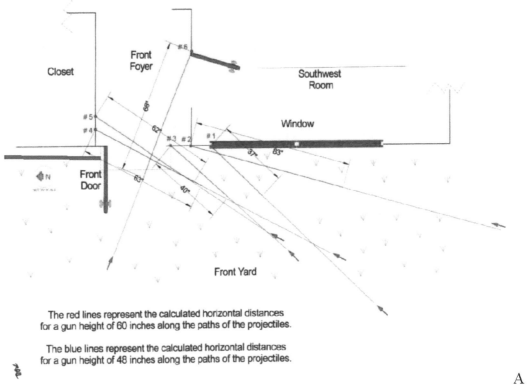

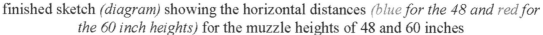

The red lines represent the calculated horizontal distances
for a gun height of 60 inches along the paths of the projectiles.

The blue lines represent the calculated horizontal distances
for a gun height of 48 inches along the paths of the projectiles.

A
finished sketch *(diagram)* showing the horizontal distances *(blue for the 48 and red for the 60 inch heights)* for the muzzle heights of 48 and 60 inches

Hints for solving assignment 16 by calculations

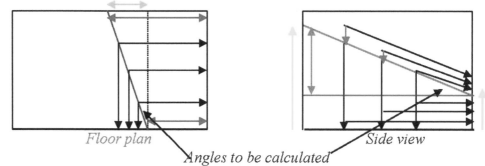

1.0 Start with the floor plan view of the room
2.0 Determine the difference between the two horizontal distances *(the green arrows)*
3.0 Use that distance *(orange arrows)* and the width of the room to calculate the horizontal distance *(the blue line)* and the two angles of that right angled triangle
4.0 Determine the difference in heights of the two ends of the strings *(the yellow arrows)*
5.0 Use the **blue** line and the difference in the heights *(the brown arrows)* to calculate the length of the string *(the red line)* and the two angles of the 2nd right angled triangle
6.0 Use the calculated angles, the length of the **string** and the length of the **blue** line to **calculate** the horizontal distances along the **blue** line, the distances along the **string** and the horizontal distances to the walls for the heights of 48, 54 and 60 inches *(The angles and the distances to be calculated are indicated by the black arrows)*

122

A. *Determine the <u>slope</u> (downward angle) of the string by the following methods*
- **1.0 Protractor**
- **2.0 Scaled drawings**
- **3.0 Smart level, Smart laser and or Laser trac**
- **4.0 Angle finder**
- **5.0 Calculations**

B. *Determine the <u>horizontal angle</u> of the string by the following methods*
- **1.0 Protractor**
- **2.0 Scaled drawings**
- **3.0 Calculations**

C. *Determine the <u>horizontal distances</u> from the wall at the lower end of the string to the heights of 48, 54 and 60 inches (above the floor) by the following methods*
- **1.0 Measurements**
- **2.0 Scaled drawings**
- **3.0 Calculations**

D. *Determine the <u>distances</u> (hypotenuses) from the lower end along the string to the same heights of 48, 54 and 60 inches above the floor*
- **1.0 Measurements**
- **2.0 Scaled drawings**
- **3.0 Calculations**

E. *Determine the <u>shortest distances</u> (perpendicular distances) to wall S for the heights of 48, 54 and 60 inches above the floor by the following methods*
- **1.0 Measurements**
- **2.0 Scaled drawings**
- **3.0 Calculations**

F. *Determine the <u>corresponding horizontal distances</u> parallel to wall S from the lower end of the string to the same heights of 48, 54 and 60 inches by the following methods*
- **1.0 Measurements**
- **2.0 Scaled drawings**
- **3.0 Calculations**

Compare the results in each category for the different methods

<u>Note</u>: *The actual measurements would involve more than one individual and would not be as accurate as the scaled drawings or the calculations*

Draw your rough sketches and do your calculations for the classroom assignment on this page

Assignment #16 – Vehicle with numerous bullet holes

Outside Assignment

Attach one end of a string to the left front quarter panel of a vehicle

Stretch the string as much as possible and attach the other end to an extended tripod or a fixed object about seven (7) feet above the ground.

Document the assignment with photographs, rough sketches and notes.
Complete the six (6) parts of the assignment as listed below the diagram.

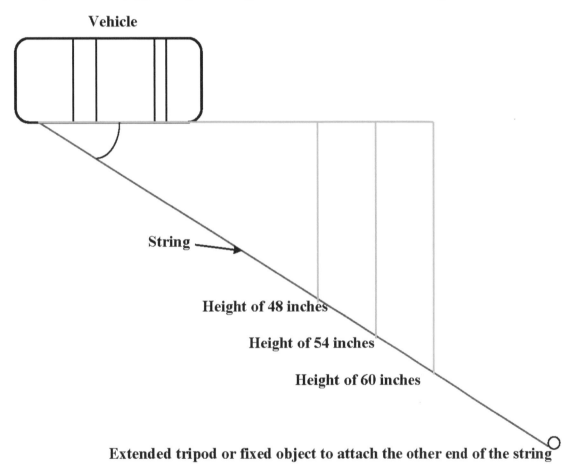

Vehicle

String

Height of 48 inches

Height of 54 inches

Height of 60 inches

Extended tripod or fixed object to attach the other end of the string

Determine the following from the string that was attached to the vehicle:

1.0 **The slope or downward angle of the string to the horizontal plane**
2.0 **The horizontal angle to the right of the string**
3.0 **The horizontal distances below** *the string* **for the heights of 48, 54 and 60 inches**
4.0 **The distances along** *the string* **for the heights of 48, 54 and 60 inches**
5.0 **The shortest or the perpendicular horizontal distances to the vehicle or the extended blue line for the heights of 48, 54 and 60 inches** *(the three green lines)*
6.0 **The horizontal distances along the side of the vehicle for the same heights** *(blue line)*

Assignment 16 continued – Calculate *the distances* for questions 3 and 5 by calculations using the same vertical and horizontal bullet impact angles and muzzle heights of 48, 54 and 60 inches *(examples below)*

Information that would needed to solve the problem:

Height of the location of the attached string *(bullet entrance hole)* = _____ inches

Horizontal distance from the string to the back of the vehicle = _____ inches

Documentation of the height of the bullet hole in the right front door of the truck

Documentation of the downward impact angle of the path of the bullet

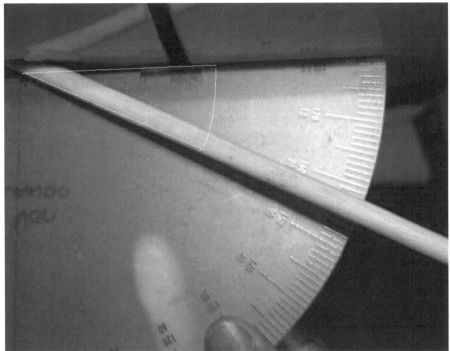

Documentation of the right horizontal impact angle of the path of the bullet

Always document the vehicle with photographs, rough sketches and notes
Calculation of the horizontal distances of the muzzle for a height of 56 inches

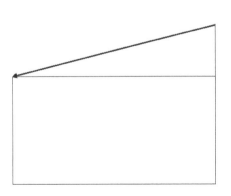

- Available information:
  - Height of bullet hole = **43.75 inches**
  - Height of the muzzle = **56 inches**
  - Downward impact angle = **5.9 degrees**

  Information to determine the formula to be used:
  - Opposite side or difference in heights **(56 – 44.75) inches = 11.25 inches**
  - Adjacent side or the distance from the muzzle to the hole = **?**
  - Impact angle = **5.9 degrees**

  Formula to be used:
  Tangent of 5.9 degrees = opposite side / adjacent side

Calculation of the horizontal distance of the muzzle for a height of 56 inches cont'd

- Making what to be determined the subject of the equation:
- **Tan 5.9 degrees = opp. side / adj side**
  - *Cross multiply because of the = sign or the equation*
- Tan 5.9 degrees x adj. side = opp. side
  - *Dividing each side of the equation by the tan of 5.9 degrees*
- **Adj. side = opp. side / tan of 5.9 degrees**
- **Calculation:**
- Adj. side or horizontal distance from the muzzle to the hole = **opp. side** or the difference in heights / tan of 5.9 degrees

- Horizontal distance:
  = opp. side / tan of 5.9 degrees
  = 11.25 inches / 0.103
  = 109.22 inches
  = 9.10 feet

Conclusion:

At a muzzle height of 56.0 inches and a downward angle of 5.9 degrees the muzzle of the gun was approximately 9.10 feet from the truck along the path of the bullet

Note: *The horizontal distance from the muzzle to the truck would change if the height of the muzzle of the gun was different*

Calculation of the horizontal perpendicular distance of the muzzle for a muzzle height of 56 inches

- Other calculations:

  - The horizontal distances from the muzzle of the gun to the respective bullet holes with a downward impact could be calculated with the same formula

  Distance = opp. side / tan of angle

  - The muzzle heights would be different for those bullet holes with an upward impact angle

- **Other calculations:**

  - *The perpendicular horizontal distances to the truck for the determined horizontal distances could be calculated using the sine ratio*

Example:

- Opp. side or horizontal perpendicular distances = ?
- Hypotenuse or calculated horizontal distance
- Horizontal impact angle

Formula:

Opp. side = hypotenuse x sin of the horizontal impact angle

= *109.2 inches x sin 25 degrees*
= *109.2 x 0.423*
= *46.1 inches*

128

Information needed to determine the location of the muzzle
(Bullet hole in the hood of the vehicle)

1.0 The location of the bullet hole in the hood *(The distances to the front, rear, right and left sides of the hood)*

2.0 The height of the bullet hole above the ground

3.0 The horizontal distance from the bullet hole to the front of the van below the path of the bullet *(Necessary to calculate the distances from the muzzle of the gun to the bullet hole and the front of the van)*

4.0 The downward and the right horizontal bullet impact angles

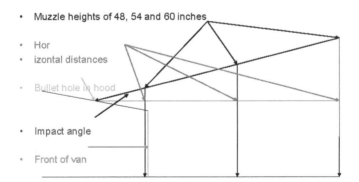

- Muzzle heights of 48, 54 and 60 inches
- Hor
- izontal distances
- Bullet hole in hood
- Impact angle
- Front of van

- Information to calculate the horizontal distances from the muzzle of the gun to the bullet hole in the hood
- The height of the bullet hole in the hood = **44 inches**
- The downward or the bullet impact angle to the horizontal plane = **19 degrees**
- The muzzle heights = **48, 54 and 60 inches**
- The horizontal distance below the path the bullet path = **13 inches**

- Information to determine the only trigonometric formula that could be used:
- The opposite sides *(The muzzle heights – The height of the bullet hole)*
- The angle to be used *(The impact angle to the horizontal plane)*
- The adjacent sides *(The horizontal distances for the corresponding muzzle heights)*

Formula: The tangent of 19 degrees = The opposite side / the adjacent side
or **the adjacent side** = The opposite side / the tangent of 19 degrees

* 48 inches muzzle height
- The horizontal distance from the muzzle of the gun to the front of the van
= *(The difference in heights / the tangent of 19 degrees) – 13 inches*
= *(48 – 44) inches / the tan of 19 degrees – 13 inches*
= *4 inches / 0.344 – 13 inches*
= *(11.63 – 13.0) inches = -1.37 inches (The muzzle was over the hood)*

* 54 inches muzzle height
- The horizontal distance from the muzzle of the gun to the front of the van
= *((54 – 44) inches / the tan of 19 degrees) – 13 inches*
= *10 inches / 0.344 – 13 inches*
= *29.07 – 13.0 inches = 16.07 inches*

* 60 inches muzzle height
- The horizontal distance from the muzzle of the gun to the front of the van
= *((60 – 44) inches / the tan of 19 degrees) – 13 inches*
= *16 inches / 0.344 – 13 inches*
= *(46.51 – 13.0) inches = 33.51 inches*

<u>*Note:*</u> *The horizontal distances for any other muzzle heights could be calculated using the same formula*

* Other calculations:

- The perpendicular horizontal distances to the van for the determined horizontal distances could be calculated using the sine (sin) ratio as in the following examples

Example:
- The opposite side or horizontal perpendicular distances = ?
- The hypotenuse or calculated horizontal distances = 16.07 and 33.51 inches
- The horizontal bullet impact angle to the right = 75 degrees

Formula:
The opposite side = The hypotenuse **x** the sin of the right horizontal impact angle

* 48 inches muzzle height
No horizontal perpendicular distance could be calculated for the 48 inch height because the muzzle of the gun was determined to be over the hood of the van

* 54 inches muzzle height
The opp. side or horizontal perpendicular distances = the hypotenuse **x** the sin of the right horizontal bullet impact angle

$$= 16.07 \text{ inches } \textbf{x} \text{ the sine of 75 degrees}$$
$$= 16.07 \text{ inches } \textbf{x} \ 0.966$$
$$= 15.52 \text{ inches}$$

* 60 inches muzzle height
The opp. side or horizontal perpendicular distances = the hypotenuse x the sin of the right horizontal bullet impact angle

$$= 33.51 \text{ inches } \textbf{x} \text{ the sine of 75 degrees}$$
$$= 33.51 \text{ inches } \textbf{x} \ 0.966$$
$$= 32.37 \text{ inches}$$

Information needed to determine the location of the muzzle
(The bullet penetrated the front windshield and then impacted the driver's seat)
Information that would be necessary to document the vehicle and then calculate the location of the muzzle of the gun for the respective muzzle heights

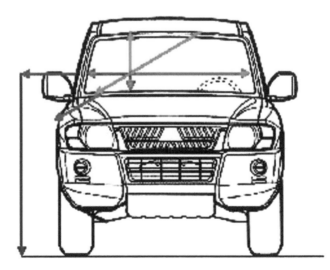

1.0   The location of the bullet hole in the right sode of the front windshield
2.0   The height of the bullet hole above the ground in the front windshield
3.0   The orientation of the bullet path through the right side of the front windshield
4.0   The horizontal distance from the front of the bumper to the bullet hole
5.0   The slope of the impacted area of the front windshield

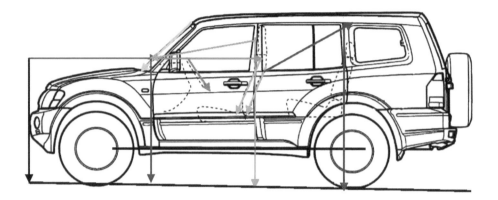

a.   The height of the extended bullet path at the back support of the driver's seat
b.   The horizontal distance from the bullet hole in the front windshield to the front of the back support of the driver's seat
c.   The location of the other impact site and impact angles of the of the path of the bullet that made the holes in the right rear section of the headliner
d.   The slope of the front and rear of the back support of the driver's seat
e.   The locations of the extended bullet path in the back support of the driver's seat from fixed locations on the dash
f.   The position and slope of the steering wheel
g.   The horizontal distance from the bullet hole in the windshield to the right and left sides of the vehicle
h.   The horizontal distance from the extended bullet path in the driver's seat to the right side of the vehicle
i.   The overall dimensions (the length, width and height) of the vehicle
j.   The type and condition of all of the tires (flat or inflated)

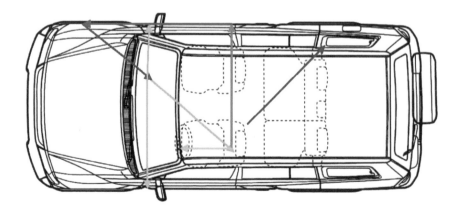

Determining the impact angles from the above information

Information that would be needed for the impact angle to the horizontal plane to later determine the horizontal distance:
Height of the bullet hole in the front windshield
Height of the second bullet hole in the driver's seat of the vehicle
The distance from the hole in the front windshield to the second bullet hole

Formula that would be used to determine the impact angle to the horizontal plane
The opposite side = the difference in the two heights
The hypotenuse = the distance from the bullet hole in the front windshield to the second bullet hole
The angle to the horizontal plane = ?
The sine of the angle to the horizontal plane = the difference in heights / the distance between the two bullet holes

= The opposite side / the hypotenuse

Formula to determine the horizontal distance (The adjacent side)
The Adjacent side = the opposite x the tangle of the angle to the horizontal plane

Determining the horizontal impact angle from the above information

Information that would be needed to determine the horizontal bullet impact angle:
The horizontal distance from the bullet hole in the front windshield to the right side of the vehicle
The horizontal distance from the bullet hole in the front of the driver's seat to the right side of the vehicle
The distance from the hole in the front windshield to the second bullet hole

Formula that would be used to determine the horizontal impact angle
The adjacent side = the difference in the two horizontal distances
The hypotenuse = the distance from the bullet hole in the front windshield to the second bullet hole
The horizontal bullet impact angle
Cosine of the horizontal bullet impact angle = the difference in the two horizontal distances / the hypotenuse

= The adjacent side / the hypotenuse

Formula to determine the horizontal distances (The opposite side)
The opposite side = the hypotenuse x the sine of the horizontal impact angle

Draw your rough sketches and do your calculations for the outside assignment below

<u>Note:</u>

1.0 The horizontal distance along the path of the bullet from where it crosses the plane of the vehicle to the impact site on the vehicle should always be determined to arrive at the horizontal distance from the vehicle.

2.0 The slope of the surface along the path of the bullet should also be determined at the impact site

Assignment 17 -Location of the muzzle of the gun by Computer drawings

The location of the muzzle of the gun and probably that of the shooter may be determined after imputing the information from the scene of the shooting in one of several computer programs

The following computer *(CADD)* generated diagrams show the possible heights of the muzzle of the gun for the three horizontal distances at the two different angles.

Fifteen (15) degrees

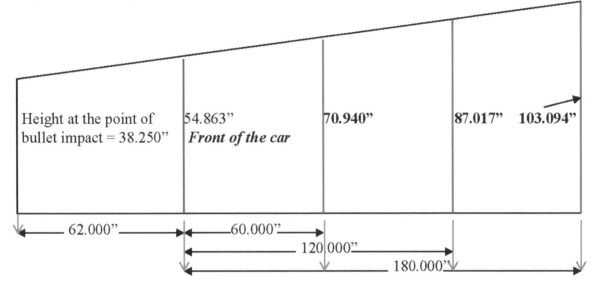

Thirteen (13) degrees

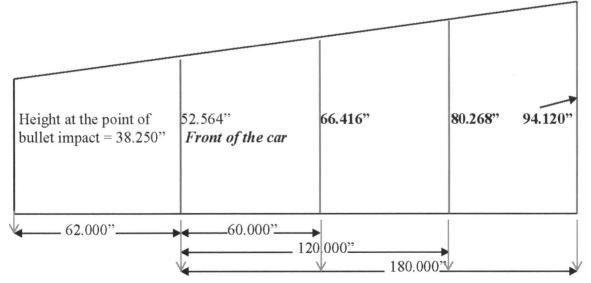

Assignment #17 continued – Location of the muzzle of the gun by Computer drawings

The location of the muzzle of the gun and probably that of the shooter may be determined after imputing the information from the scene of the shooting in one of several computer programs

Determine the heights by three methods for the corresponding horizontal distances if the height of the bullet impact to the hood was 36 inches above the ground and the distance from the front of the car was 58 inches

Fifteen (15) degrees

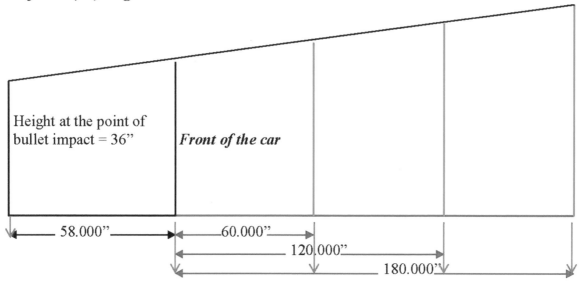

Thirteen (13) degrees

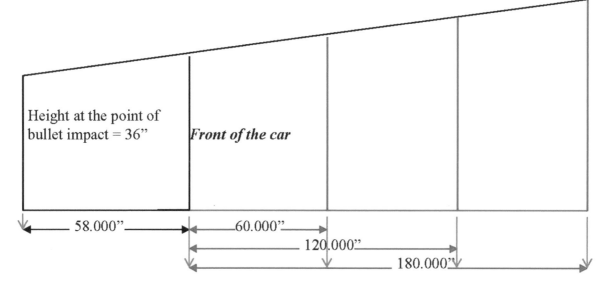

Location of the muzzle by a Protractor with a Laser

The location of the muzzle of the gun and probably that of the shooter may be determined by the use of a protractor with an attached laser
The following horizontal distances and the distances along the beam of light may be measured for each corresponding muzzle height that would be relevant to your case.

Fifteen (15) degrees

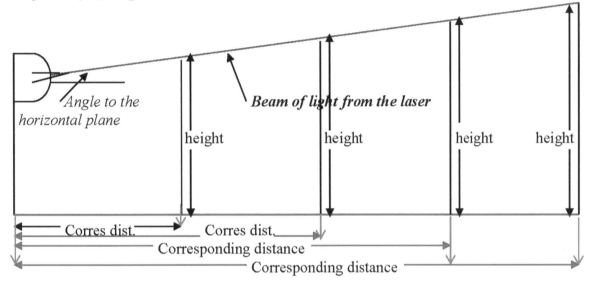

Thirteen (13) degrees

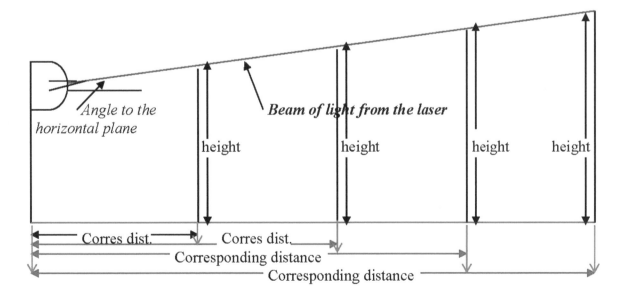

Assignment # 18 - Shooting Reconstruction Problems

Problem #1

Summary:

The female victim and three other adults were traveling up a river in a Pontoon boat when she was shot in the neck. The female victim was rushed to the Hospital where she was treated and survived her neck injury.

The suspect, who was apparently standing on the river bank, alleged that he was shooting at some ducks in the water that were about 50 feet or less away from him.

Three witnesses reportedly observed the boat in three different locations at the time of the shooting.

Available Information:

The height of the victim's injury *(neck)* above the water was approximately **60.0 inches**
The height of the muzzle of the weapon above the water was approximately **108.5 inches**
The reported distances from the muzzle of the gun to the three observed (3) locations of the boat were approximately:

1.0 - **189.64 feet**   *2.0* - **353.32 feet**   *3.0* - **439.48 feet**

Reported type of weapon – a .22 caliber rifle
It is reported that a bullet could be deflected off the surface of water if the maximum bullet impact angle was approximately **6.0 degrees or less.**
It is also reported that the angle of deflection is usually greater than the impact angle and that the maximum angle of deflection about **7.0 degrees or less**.
The suspect stated that he was shooting at some ducks which were less than **50.0 feet** away from him.

Problems to be solved:

A. Determine the *horizontal distance* from the muzzle of the gun to the bullet impact site in the water at the maximum bullet impact angle of **6.0 degrees.**

B. Determine the *horizontal distance* from the bullet exit site in the water to the bullet impact site in the victim's neck at the maximum angle of deflection angle of **7.0 degrees.** *(Assume that the bullet traveled in a straight line from the water to the victim's neck)*

C. Could the deflection be possible if the ducks were **50** feet or less away from the shooter?

D. Determine the *downward angles to the horizontal plane* and *the distances traveled* for each location of the boat *assuming* that the bullet traveled in a straight line to the victim without any drop-off

Draw your rough sketches and do your calculations for the shooting reconstruction for problem #1 below

Shooting Reconstruction Problem #2

Summary:

The victim who was traveling southbound in the far right lane of the three (3) lane interstate highway was shot in the chest through the driver's door just before he was about to get off on to the exit ramp to his right.

The victim apparently drove off on the exit ramp then apparently lost control of his vehicle as a result of the injuries of his gunshot wound. He then ran off the exit ramp and slammed into a tree where he was later found deceased in his truck.

Available information:

Height of the bullet entrance hole in the driver's door above the road   **= 48.0 inches**
Upward bullet impact angle to the horizontal plane   **= 7.0 degrees**
Horizontal impact angle to the left when facing the driver's door   **= 49.0 degrees**

Problems:

A.   Determine the *horizontal distance* below the extended path of the bullet from the hole in the driver's door of the truck to the road. *(assume that the road is level)*

B.   Determine the *perpendicular horizontal distance* from the hole in the driver's door of the truck to that location on road from the above assignment.

C.   Determine the *perpendicular horizontal distance* from the hole in the driver's of the truck to the muzzle of the gun if it was approximately **36.0 inches** above the road? *This means that the bottom of right door window would have been about **36.0 inches** above the road.*

D.   Determine the *perpendicular horizontal distances* if the heights of the muzzle were greater than 36.0 inches above the road *(39.0 inches, 42.0 inches and 45.0 inches)*.

Interstate

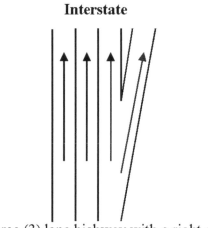

Three (3) lane highway with a right exit ramp

Draw your rough sketches and do your calculations for the shooting reconstruction for problem #2 below

Shooting Reconstruction Problem #3

Summary:

In a drive-by shooting incident one of the shots that were fired at the vehicle was deflected off of the driver's door. This bullet impact to the driver's door created an indentation with a downward angle to the horizontal plane.

Available information:

Height of the center of the indentation in the driver's door	= **18.25 inches**
Downward angle to the horizontal plane of the indentation	= **25 degrees**
Horizontal bullet impact angle to the right when facing the driver's side of the car	= **15 degrees**
Distance from the bullet impact site to the back of the vehicle	= **65 inches**

Problems:

A. Determine the horizontal distances *(orange lines in the diagram below)* for the muzzle heights of **48, 54, and 60 inches.**

B. Determine the perpendicular horizontal distances *(green lines in the diagram below)* from the driver's side of the car for the same muzzle heights.

C. Determine the horizontal distances *(blue lines in the diagram below)* along the driver's side of the car from the bullet impact site to the location of the perpendicular horizontal distance for the same muzzle heights *(same as assignment #16)*.

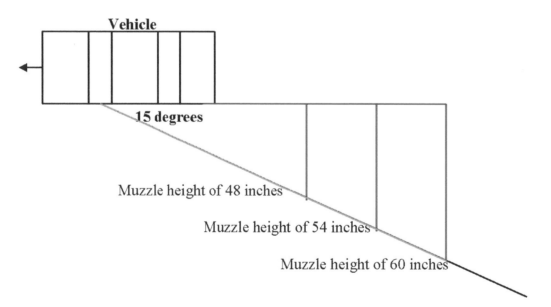

Draw your rough sketches and do your calculations for shooting the reconstruction for problem #3 below

Shooting Reconstruction Problem #4

Summary:

The female victim, who was in the kitchen, was upright and facing the suspect when she was shot in the chest. The bullet exited the victim's back and got lodged in the overhead cabinet behind her where it was later recovered. The victim was shot a second time *(contact shot)* in the head as she was falling to the floor. The second shot created back and side impact blood spatter on the front of the refrigerator door.

Available Information:

Upward impact angle of the horizontal of the path of the bullet   = 15.0 degrees

Height of the victim's bullet entrance hole   = 57.0 inches

Assume that the suspect's back was against the wall and that the muzzle of the gun was about 24.0 inches from the same wall (horizontal distance)

Problems: *(Please see the diagrams on the next two pages)*

A. Determine the *horizontal distance* from the victim's bullet entrance hole to the wall at the back of the suspect

B. Determine the *distance traveled* from the victim's bullet entrance wound along the extended path of the bullet in the opposite direction to the wall at the back of the suspect

C. Determine the *height of the muzzle of the gun* at the time of the first shot.

D. Determine the *distance* the bullet traveled from the muzzle of the gun to the victim's entrance bullet hole

E. Determine the *horizontal distance* from the muzzle of the gun to the victim's bullet entrance hole.

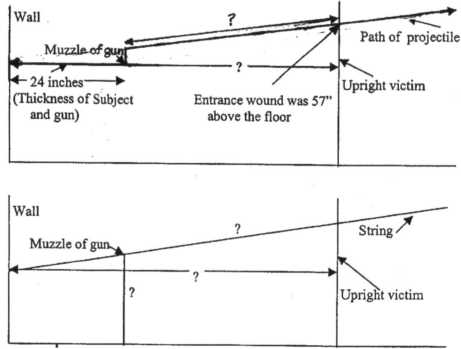

Diagrams of the path of the bullet and the distances (**?**) to be calculated or drawn to scale

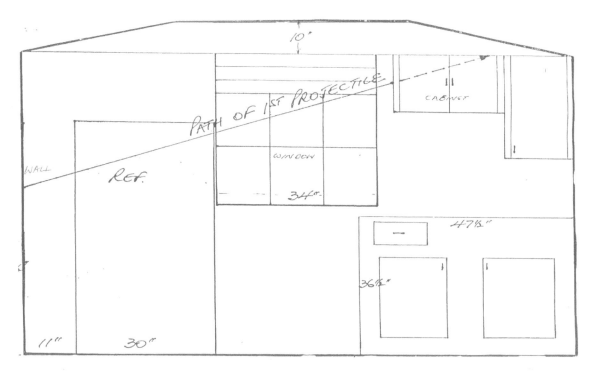

Diagram of the north wall of the kitchen to show the extended upward path of the bullet

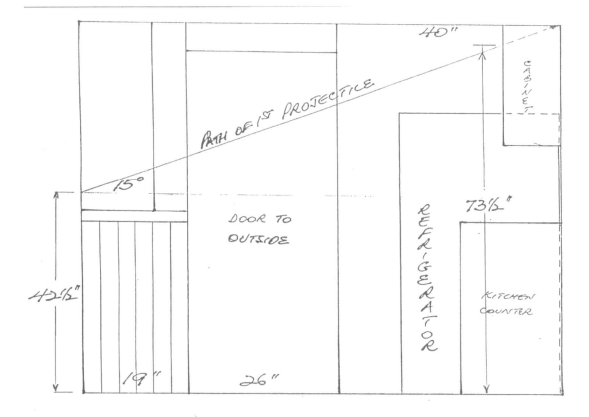

Diagram of the west wall of the kitchen to show the extended path of the bullet

Draw your rough sketches and do your calculations for the shooting reconstruction for problem #4 below

Shooting Reconstruction Problem #5

Summary:

The female victim was seated on the bed when she was shot in the top right side of the chest near the neck. The bullet exited the lower left side of her body and penetrated the head board to her left. The ME reported that no apparent defection of the bullet was observed in the victim's body.

The suspect alleged that he was reaching for a gun which was on a shelf at the left corner of the wall at the foot of the bed when facing the bed.

Available Information:

Downward bullet impact angle to the horizontal plane relative to the upper portion of the victim's body being in an upright position   = 50.0 degrees
Height of the seated victim's bullet entrance hole to the chest   = 43 inches
Allowance in the downward impact angle to the horizontal plane to compensate for movement of the victim's upper body to the left or right   *= 10 degrees*

PLEASE see the diagram on the following page

Problems:

A.   **Bullet impact angle to the horizontal plane of 40 degrees**
    Determine the *heights of the muzzle of the gun* for the **horizontal** distances of **2, 3, 4 and 5 feet.**
    Determine the *distances traveled (the hypotenuses)* from the muzzle of the gun to the victim's bullet entrance wound for the same horizontal distances.

B.   **Bullet impact angle to the horizontal plane of 50 degrees**
    Determine the *heights of the muzzle of the gun* for the **horizontal** distances of **2, 3, 4 and 5 feet.**
    Determine the *distances traveled (the hypotenuses)* from the muzzle of the gun to the victim's bullet entrance wound for the same horizontal distances.

C.   **Bullet impact angle to the horizontal plane of 60 degrees**
    Determine the *heights of the muzzle of the gun* for the **horizontal** distances of **2, 3, 4 and 5 feet.**
    Determine the *distances traveled (the hypotenuses)* from the muzzle of the gun to the victim's bullet entrance wound for the same horizontal distances.

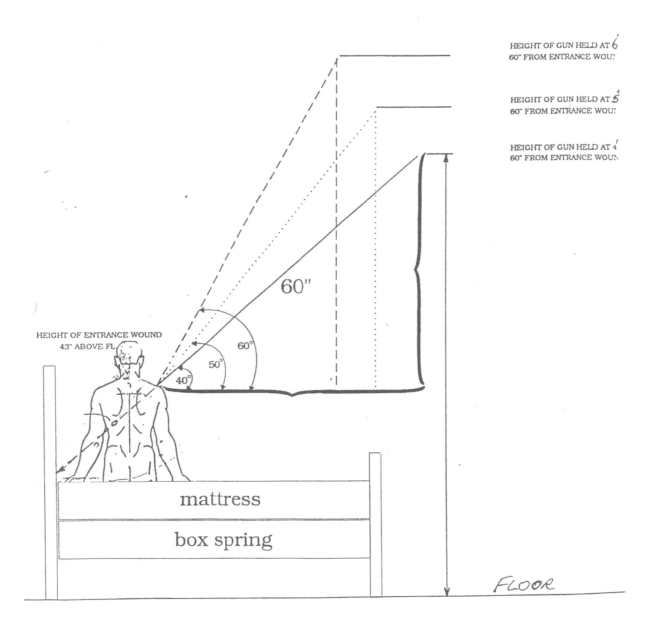

HEIGHT OF GUN HELD AT 6'
60" FROM ENTRANCE WOUND

HEIGHT OF GUN HELD AT 5'
60" FROM ENTRANCE WOUND

HEIGHT OF GUN HELD AT 4'
60" FROM ENTRANCE WOUND

60"

HEIGHT OF ENTRANCE WOUND
43" ABOVE FLOOR

60°

50°

40°

mattress

box spring

FLOOR

Diagram showing the relative location of the victim at the time she was shot in the top right area of her chest.

The three different lines represent the three impact angles of 40, 50 and 60 degrees to the horizontal plane for the possible movement of the victim to the left or the right.

Draw your rough sketches and do your calculations for the shooting reconstruction for problem #5 below

Shooting Reconstruction Problem #6

Summary:

The victim and the suspect were arguing in the bedroom of their trailer home. The suspect discharged his shotgun as the victim left the bedroom and walked around the dividing wall. The shot traveled in an upward direction through the dividing wall and some of the pellets penetrated the victim's head and killed him. A few of the pellets were deflected upward off the victim's head into the dropped ceiling tiles.

Available Information:

Height of the bullet entrance hole on the bedroom side of the wall	= 45.5 inches
Height of the bullet exit hole on the other side of the wall	= 46.5 inches
Distance the shot traveled through the wall	= 3.25 inches
Height of the bullet entrance wound to the then upright victim's head	= 68.0 inches
Horizontal distance of the bullet hole in the bedroom side of the wall	= 15 .0 inches
Horizontal distance of the bullet exit hole in the other side of the wall	= 15.0 inches

Problems:

A.   Is there any significance to the two *horizontal distances* being the same?

B.   Determine the *thickness of the dividing wall* with the entrance and exit holes.

C.   Determine the *upward impact angle* to the horizontal plane.

D.   Determine the *location of the upright victim* relative to the side wall with the exit hole.

E.   Determine the *distance traveled* from the exit hole in the wall to the victim's forehead.

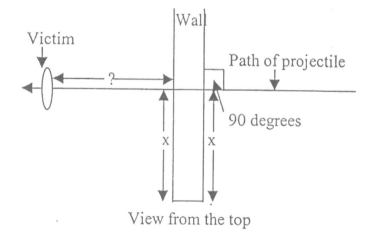

Diagram showing the suspected path of the bullet through a section of the dividing wall
Note: *The two xs indicated that two horizontal distances were the same.*

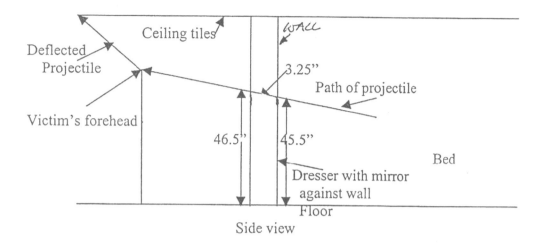

Diagram showing the suspected path of the bullet through the dividing wall

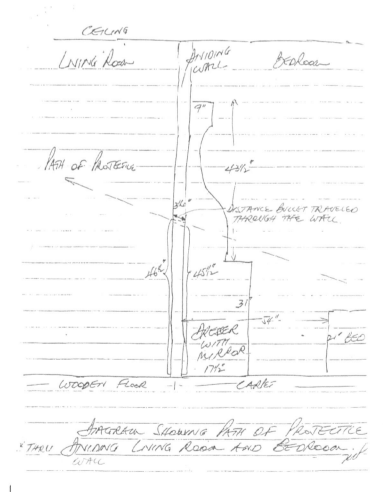

Rough sketch a section of the bedroom and the path of the bullet through the wall

Draw your rough sketches and do your calculations for the shooting reconstruction for problem #6 below

Shooting Reconstruction Problem #7

Summary:

The subject fired two shots into the hood of the vehicle that was apparently going to run him over. Several other shots were fired at the vehicle after he was struck by the vehicle and fell to the ground.

Available Information:

Bullet hole #1 on the passenger's side of the hood

Downward bullet impact angle to the horizontal plane	= 13.0 degrees
Height of the bullet hole above the ground	= 38.25 inches
Horizontal distance below the path of the bullet from the bullet hole to the front of the car	= 62.0 inches

Bullet hole #2 on the driver's side of the hood

Downward bullet impact angle to the horizontal plane	= 10.0 degrees
Height of the bullet hole above the ground	= 37.50 inches
Horizontal distance below the path of the bullet from the bullet hole to the front of the car	= 46.5 inches

Problems:

Determine the *locations of the muzzle of the gun* relative to the front of the car for both shots at the muzzle heights of 60, 65 and 70 inches.

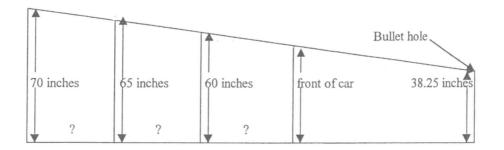

Diagram of the suspected path of the bullet to the right side of the hood of the car

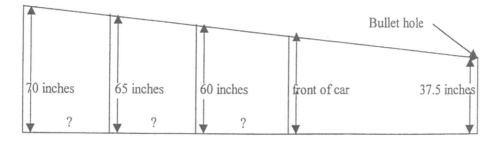

Diagram of the suspected path of the bullet to the left side of the hood of the car

153

Draw your rough sketches and do your calculations for the shooting reconstruction for problem #7 below

Shooting Reconstruction Problem #8

Summary:

The victim was allegedly shot in the head as she was ironing her clothes to go to work. She was apparently left on the floor where she fell for some time. The suspect later fired a shot in the refrigerator door and claimed that this occurred as both of them were struggling for the gun near the ironing board.

A dowel rod was placed in the bullet hole and a string was attached to it and extended along the most likely path to the ceiling. Measurements for the different heights and distances along the string from the wall and iron were taken from the string and sent to me for review.

Note: *The horizontal distances should have been taken (measured) as a part of the crime scene documentation and those measurements should have been used to determine the respective heights and distances traveled if needed.*

Available Information:

Downward bullet impact angle to the horizontal plane   = 23 degrees
Height of the bullet entrance hole in the refrigerator door   = 30.625 inches
Measurements from the string on the diagram

Problems: *(Please see the diagrams on the next page)*

1.0   Determine the ***horizontal distances*** from the refrigerator door to the areas with the following listed heights of 57, 74.5, 83 and 96 inches.

2.0   Determine the ***distances*** along the string to the refrigerator door for the following locations.

    a. The back of the partial wall

    b. The front or closer side of the ironing board

    c. The rear or far side of the ironing board

    d. The location on the ceiling where the extended string was attached

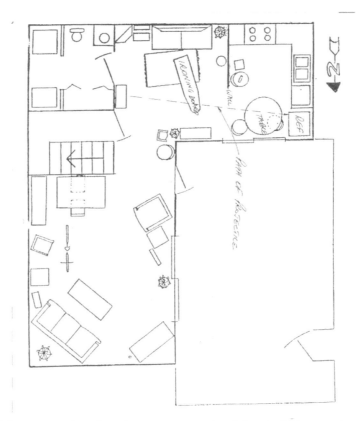

Floor plan of the scene showing the suspect path of the 2nd shot to the refrigerator door

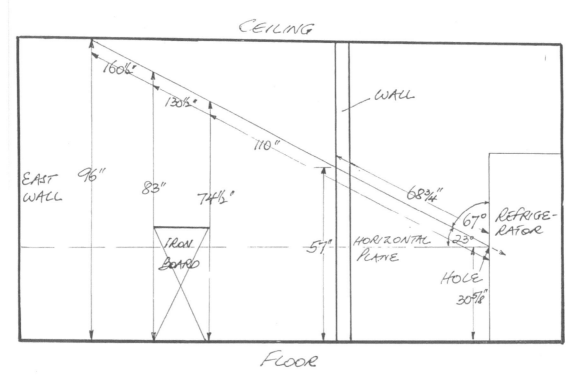

Diagram of the extended string with the with the respective heights and the corresponding distances along the string

Draw your rough sketches and do your calculations for the shooting reconstruction for problem #8 below

Shooting Reconstruction Problem #9

Summary:

The female subject who was slightly bent over at the top of the stairs was shot once in the chest after firing several shots in the direction where the shooter was located.
Several other shots were apparently fired by the subject from other locations of the home with other guns before she was finally shot once.
The bullet exited the body (back) after being slightly deflected upward and was recovered from the wall at the back of the subject where it was lodged.

Available Information:

Height of the muzzle of the gun	= 30 inches
Height of the bullet entrance wound in the subject's chest	= 48.25 inches
Height of the impact site in the wall at the back of the subject	= 62.0 inches
Height of the floor of the room above the ground	= 25.0 inches
Horizontal distance below the path of the bullet after it exited the body	= *19.0 feet*
Horizontal distance from the muzzle to the subject	= *117.75 feet*
Horizontal distance from the muzzle to the impact site in the wall	= *136.75 feet*

Problem:

A. Determine the *horizontal distance from the muzzle of the gun* to the bullet entrance hole in the subject's chest if the bullet was not deflected? *That is if the path was extended backward from the impact site in the wall at the back of the victim.*

Diagram of the suspected path of the bullet and the deflection after exiting the body

Diagram of the suspected path of the bullet through the body without any deflection

Draw your rough sketches and do your calculations for the shooting reconstruction for problem #9 below

Shooting Reconstruction Problem #10

Summary:

The suspect fired three shots into the victim's moving vehicle. It is believed that the driver was driving backward to avoid the shooter.

Available Information:

Bullet hole #1
Height of the bullet impact entrance hole above the ground	= 36.5 inches
Downward bullet impact angle to the horizontal plane	= 9.0 degrees
Horizontal bullet impact angle to center of the hood	= 17.0 degrees

Bullet hole #2
Height of the bullet impact entrance hole above the ground	= 37.5 inches
Downward bullet impact angle to the horizontal plane	= 16.5 degrees
Horizontal bullet impact angle to center of the hood	= 29.7 degrees

Bullet hole #3
Height of the bullet impact entrance hole above the ground	= 42.25 inches
Downward bullet impact angle to the horizontal plane	= 38.1 degrees
Horizontal bullet impact angle to center of the hood	= 16 to 20 degrees

Problems: *(Please see the diagrams on the next page)*

A.   Determine the *horizontal distances* from the muzzle of the gun to the three bullet holes for the muzzle heights of 48 and 60 inches.   .

B.   What do the backward movement of the car and the stationary location of the shooter indicate about the sequence of the three shots?

C.   Determine the *distances traveled* from the muzzle of the gun to the three bullet impact sites in the car.

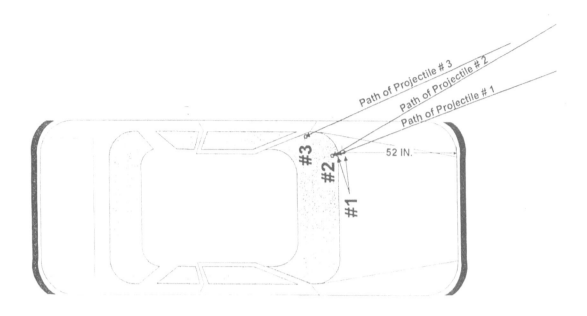

Diagram showing the horizontal impact angles to the driver's side of the car

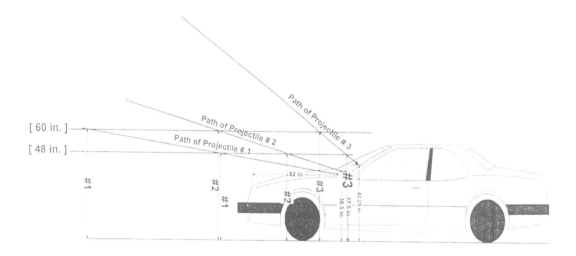

Diagram showing the downward bullet impact angles to the horizontal plane

161

Draw your rough sketches and do your calculations for the shooting reconstruction for problem #10 below

Shooting Reconstruction Problem #11

Summary:

The victim, who was bent over in booth #2 with her back to the suspect as she was cleaning the table, was shot by the suspect who seated in the far seat of booth #1. The suspect claimed that she was looking for something in her purse which was on the seat next to her when her 45 caliber revolver that was in her purse accidentally discharged and struck the bent over victim in the back. The bullet exited the victim and penetrated the dividing wall between the dining area and the kitchen.

Available Information:

Height of the table of the booth above the floor	= 30.25 inches
Height of the seat of the booth above the floor	= 17.0 inches
Upward bullet impact angle to the horizontal plane	= 1.4 to 2.3 degrees

Other information available from the sketches below and on the next page

Problems:

Determine *the muzzle heights* along the center of the projected bullet path for the following locations.

A.   The side of table #1 that was closer to the suspect

B.   The center of table #1

C.   The side of table #1 that was further away from the suspect

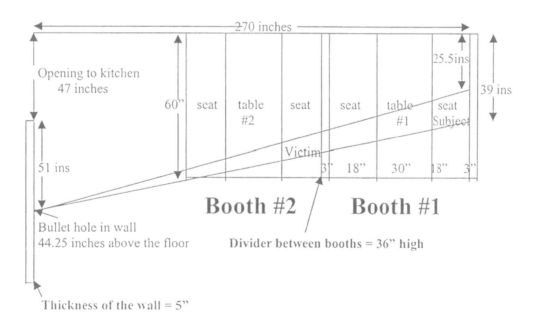

Sketch of the suspected area of the path of the bullet and the floor plan of the scene with measurements

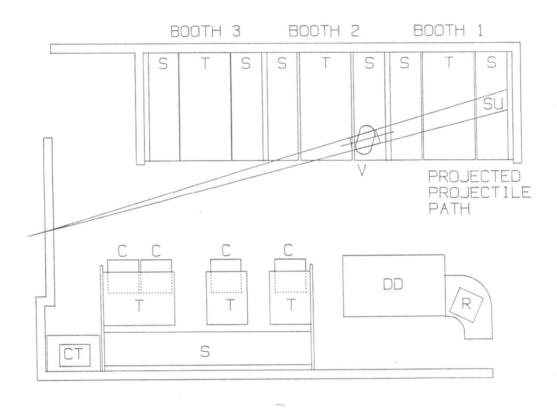

Diagram of the suspected area of the path of the bullet and the floor plan of the scene

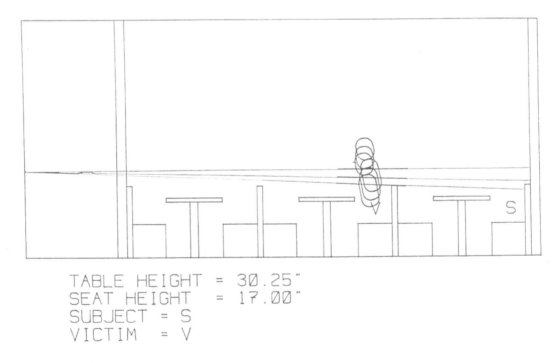

TABLE HEIGHT = 30.25"
SEAT HEIGHT = 17.00"
SUBJECT = S
VICTIM = V

Diagram showing the vertical plane and the two suspected paths of the bullet for the two upwards angles of 1.4 and 2.3 degrees to the horizontal plane

Draw your rough sketches and do your calculations for the shooting reconstruction for problem #11below

Shooting Reconstruction Problem #12

Summary:

The victim was shot twice in the left forearm and the left side of the back near the armpit as he sat in the driver's seat of his car. He was apparently talking to someone on his cell phone at the time of the incident.

Available Information:

From the Medical Examiner's Office

Height of the entrance wound above the heel to the left side of the back	= 53 inches
Height of the corresponding exit wound above the heel on the right side	= 45 inches
Distance the bullet traveled through the body	= 22 inches

From the scene

Height of the bottom of the driver's door window with the glass down	= 36 inches
Height of the entrance wound when the victim was seated in the driver's seat	= 38 inches
Horizontal distance between the wound and the outside of the driver's door	= 5 inches

Problems:

A.   Determine the *downward bullet impact angle* through the victim's body relative to it being in an upright position.

B.   Determine the *horizontal distances* along the path of the bullet from the muzzle of the gun to the entrance wound in the left side of the victim's back at the muzzle heights of 48, 60 and 72 inches.

C.   Determine the *distances traveled* from the muzzle of the gun to the entrance wound in the left side of the victim's back at the muzzle heights of 48, 60 and 72 inches.

D.   Determine the *horizontal distances* along the paths of the bullet from the muzzle of the gun at the height of the bottom of the drive's door window for the muzzle heights of 48, 60 and 72 inches.

E.   How will the following be affected if the victim leaned to his right but the muzzle of the gun was held in the same position?
   a.   The angle through the body
   b.   The horizontal distance
   c.   The distance traveled by the bullet

F.   How will the following be affected if the shooter was closer to the door?
   a.   The angle through the body
   b.   The horizontal distances
   c.   The distances traveled by the bullet

Draw your rough sketches and do your calculations for the shooting reconstruction foe problem #12 below

Shooting Reconstruction Problem #13

Summary:

The victim was shot in the upper right side of her chest and the projectile exited her back near her spinal column. The victim was partially paralyzed as a result of her injuries and was unable to walk after being shot.

Available Information:

From the victim

Height of the victim's bullet entrance wound	= 54.5 inches
Height of the victim's bullet exit wound	= 51.5 inches
Distance the bullet traveled through the body	= 6.5 inches

From the scene

Horizontal distance from the muzzle of the gun to the wall in which the bullet was located
= 254 .0 inches

Horizontal distance along the path of the bullet from the muzzle of the gun to center of the pool of blood on the floor = 71.0 inches

Height of the bullet hole in the south wall which was made by the bullet after it exited the victim's body = 53.5 inches

Problems: *(Please see the diagrams on the next two pages)*

A. Determine the ***downward bullet impact angle*** to the horizontal plane through the victim's if she was in an upright position.

B. Determine the ***impact angles to the horizontal plane*** if the bullet traveled uninterrupted to the south wall from the muzzle heights of 30 and 36 inches.

C. How much the victim's body would have been bent over for the bullet entrance and exit wounds to be in the path of the bullet for the muzzle heights 30 and 36 inches?

D. Determine the ***maximum horizontal distances*** from the muzzle of the gun to the victim's bullet entrance wound if she was bent over and the bullet passed through her body from the muzzle heights 30 and 36 inches.

E. Determine the ***maximum distances traveled*** by the bullet from the muzzle of the gun to the victim's bullet entrance wound if she was bent over and the bullet passed through her body from the 30 and 36 inches muzzle heights.

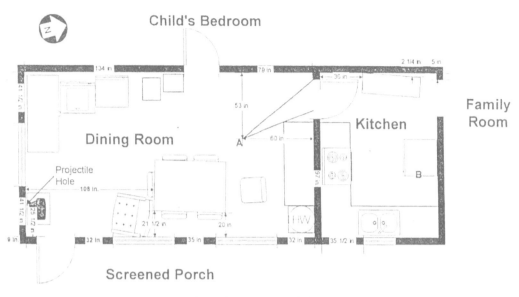

Diagram of the floor plan of the scene

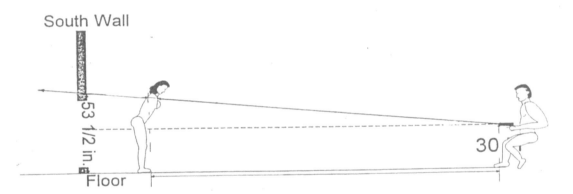

Diagram showing the approximate position and location of the victim if she was shot shortly after entering the front door from a muzzle height of 30 inches

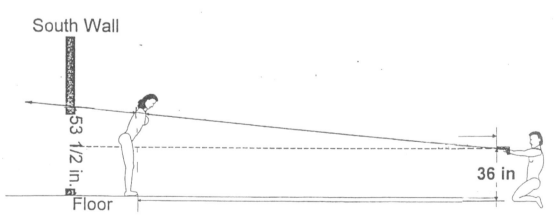

Diagram showing the approximate position and location of the victim if she was shot shortly after entering the front door from a muzzle height of 36 inches

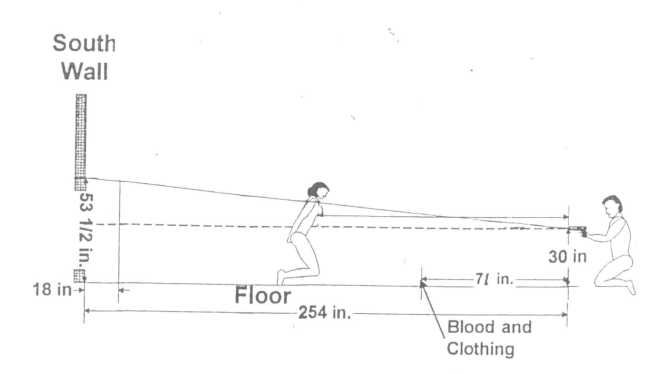

Diagram showing the approximate position and location of the victim if she was shot near the pool of blood on the floor from a muzzle height of 30 inches

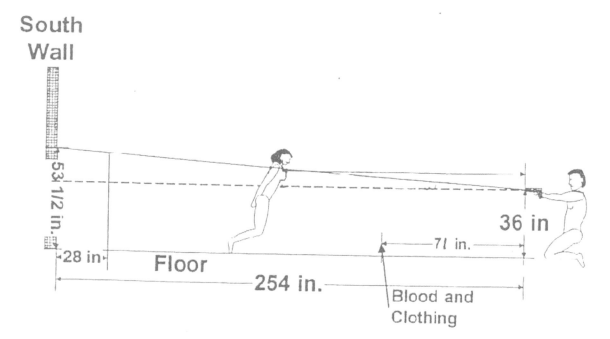

Diagram showing the approximate position and location of the victim if she was shot near the pool of blood on the floor from a muzzle height of 36 inches

170

Draw your rough sketches and do your calculation for the shooting reconstruction for problem #13 below

Shooting Reconstruction Problem #14

Summary:

The subject was accidentally shot in his right leg as he stood behind the bedroom door which opened to the outside. The bullet exited his leg and was later recovered from the carpet on the bedroom floor.

Available Information:

From the scene
Height of the bullet entrance hole in the outside of the bedroom door	= 21.25 inches
Height of the bullet exit hole in the inside of the bedroom door	= 20.50 inches
Distance the bullet traveled through the bedroom door	= 1.625 inches
Horizontal distance from the left side of the door to the entrance hole	= 11.25 inches
Horizontal distance from the left side of the door to the exit hole	= 11.75 inches
Distance from the door jamb to the edge of the partially opened door	= 18.00 inches

From the subject
Height of the bullet entrance wound in the subject's leg	= 16.00 inches

Problems:

A. Determine the *angle* at which the bedroom door was opened when the bullet penetrated the subject's leg

B. How *far* was the subject's bullet entrance hole in the leg from the partially opened bedroom door at the time of the shooting?

C. How *far* did the bullet travel from the bullet exit hole in the bedroom door to where it was found in the carpet if it was not deflected?

D. Determine the *horizontal distance* along the path of the bullet from the bullet exit hole in the bedroom door to the location in the carpet where it was located.

E. Determine the *horizontal distances* from the muzzle of the gun to the entrance bullet hole in the bedroom door for the muzzle heights of 36, 42 and 48 inches.

F. Determine the *distances traveled* from the muzzle of the gun to the entrance bullet hole in the bedroom door for the muzzle heights of 36, 42 and 48 inches.

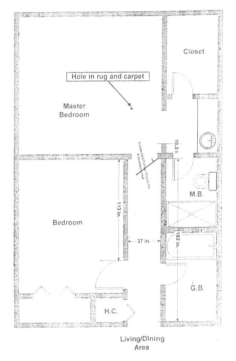

Diagram of the floor plan with measurements of a section of the house

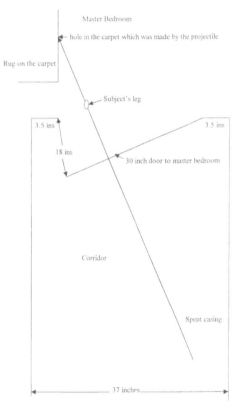

Diagram of the suspected bath of the bullet hole through the bedroom door

Draw the rough sketches and do your calculations for the shooting reconstruction for problem #14 below

Shooting Reconstruction Problem #15

Summary:

The male subject and the female victim *(girlfriend)* were in his vehicle when she received a grazing wound to the front of her head. The victim died from her injury because of the time that elapsed in getting her help. The subject according to what he allegedly told the police did not make a 911 call even though he reportedly had his cell phone with him.

He instead travel from the top of the mountain then turned right and flagged down another driver instead of turning left which would have been the shortest distance to the hospital.

Two shots were discharged from the gun which was never recovered by the police. One of the two bullet casings was recovered from the right rear passenger's foot well. One shot that grazed the victim's forehead as she was seated in the rear seat was recovered from the right rear area of the headliner near the overhead passenger's grip or holder. The other shot penetrated the right side of the front windshield then nipped the right windshield wiper and was never recovered by the police.

The subject claimed that an unknown assailant fired the two shots from the driver's side rear window which was opened **5.5 inches. The top of the driver's seat headrest was** 1.0 inch **higher than the top of the driver's side rear window.**

Vehicle with the bullet holes:
The vehicle was 1995 4-door Isuzu Trooper that was 166.5 inches long and 68.7 inches wide. **The bullet hole was 10.75 inches from the right windshield column, 4.5 inches above the bottom of the windshield; the horizontal impact angle to the left was approximately 70 degrees and was about 58 inches from the center of the front of the back support of the driver's seat.**
The horizontal impact angle of the 2nd shot was approximately 55.0 degrees to the left.

Bullet hole

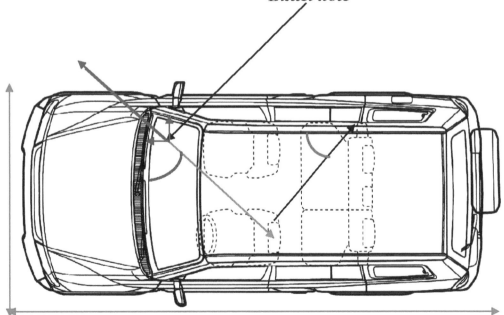

The height of the Isuzu trooper was approximately 72.8 above the ground and the
downward impact angle was approximately 21 degrees to the horizontal plane. The
height of the bullet hole was approximately 51.0 inches above the ground.

Bullet Hole

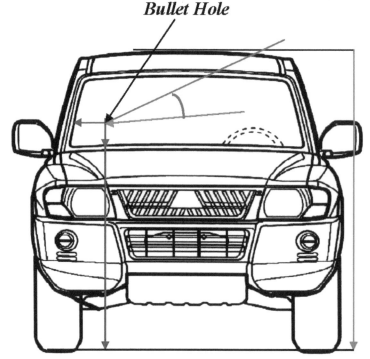

The height of the top of the opened driver's door rear window was 61.0 inches above
the ground and the window was opened 5.5 inches. The incline of the front of the back
support of the driver's seat support was approximately 73.1 degrees and the incline of
the rear of the of the back support of the driver's seat was approximately 79.6 degrees.
The upward impact angle of the 2nd bullet was approximately 40.0 degrees

Bullet Hole

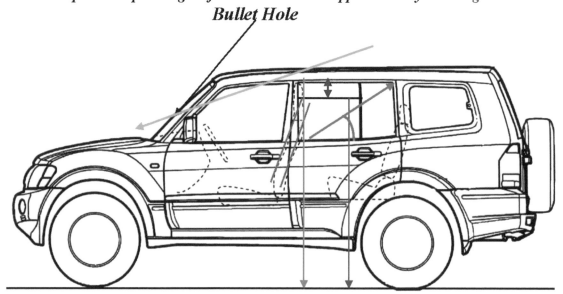

Slope of the location where the incident occurred *(vehicles are driven on the left side)*
The downward slope was approximately 3.3 degrees, **the slope to the right was approximately** 5.6 degrees **and the resultant slope was approximately** 4.5 degrees

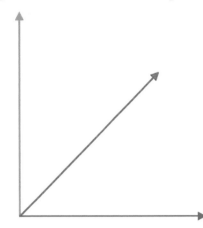

Problems:

A.   The subject claimed that an assailant fired two shot through the partially opened left rear door window of the trooper. Is it possible that the bullet which penetrated the front windshield was discharged from a firearm that was held outside of the driver's side rear window of the trooper?

B.   Would the resultant slope of the road make any difference in the determination the location of the muzzle of the firearm relative to the trooper?

C.   What was the elevation of the area of the road at the left rear corner *(driver's side)* of the trooper relative to the right front corner of the trooper as a result of the resultant slope of 4.5 degrees of the road?

D.   Calculate the *height of the muzzle* of the firearm at the front of the back support of the driver's seat if the height of the bullet hole in the right side of the front windshield was 51 inches above the ground, the horizontal distance from the bullet hole to the front of the back support of the driver's seat was 58 inches and the downward impact angle to the horizontal plane in the front windshield was 21 degrees when the trooper was on a level surface.

E.   Calculate the *horizontal distance* from the right rear corner of the back support of the driver's seat to the bullet hole in the right rear section of the headliner if the distance from the rear of the seat to the bullet hole was 47 inches and the upward impact angle to the horizontal plane was 40 degrees when the trooper was on a level surface.

F.   How the bullet would be deflected based on the photographs of the injury to the victim's forehead if she was in the rear seat when she was shot? The bullet that grazed the victim in the forehead was recovered from the right rear headliner near the passenger overhead grip or handle.

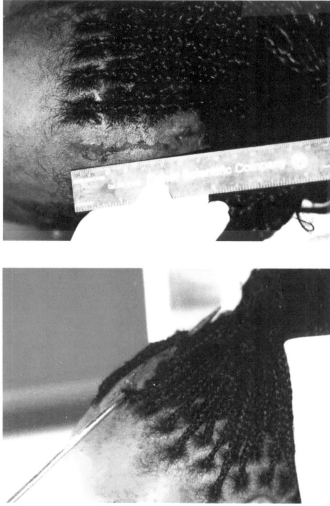

Photographs of the injury to the victim's forehead

Photograph of the string in place to show the suspected path of one of the bullets

Draw your rough sketches and do your calculations for the shooting reconstruction for problem #15 below

Answers to the Math Review and the Problems

Page 45

Angles B and C, F and G are *vertically opposite angles*.

Angles E and F, F and H, G and H, E and G are *supplementary* angles

Angles B and E *(60 and 120)*, B and H *(60 and 120)* are *supplementary*
Angles C and E *(60 and 120)*, C and H *(60 and 120)* are *supplementary*
Angles D and F *(120 and 60)*, D and G *(120 and 60)* are *supplementary*

Page 46

Angle B = *(180 - 92)* degrees = **88 degrees** *(supplementary to 92)*
Angle C = **92 degrees** *(vertically opposite to 92)*
Angle D = *(180 - 92)* degrees = **88 degrees** *(supplementary to 92)*

Angle B = **135 degrees** *(supplementary to 45)*
Angle C =   **45 degrees** *(vertically opposite to 45)*
Angle D = **135 degrees** *(supplementary to 45)*

Angle E =   **45 degrees** *(corresponding to 45)*
Angle F = 135 **degrees** *(supplementary to 135)*
Angle G =   **45 degrees** *(vertically opposite to 45)*
Angle H = **135 degrees** *(supplementary to 45)*

Page 48

Angle A = **60 degrees** *(complimentary to 30 or supplementary to 30 and B)*
Angle B = **90 degrees** *(right angle or supplementary to A and 30)*
Angle C = **60 degrees** *(corresponding to A)*
Angle D = **30 degrees** *(corresponding to 30 or supplementary to C and E)*
Angle E = **90 degrees** *(right angle or supplementary to D and C)*

Angle A = **45 degrees** *(A and B are complimentary and B is corresponding to 45)*
Angle B = **45 degrees** *(B is complimentary to A)*
Angle C = **45 degrees** *(C is complimentary to 45)*

Page 50

H3 = H1 – H2 = 40 inches – 35 inches = **5 inches**
H3 = H2 – H1 = 40 inches – 32 inches = **8 inches**

Page 52

Angle B = **65 degrees** *(180 − 50)* degrees divided by 2 or 130 degrees / 2

A + B + B are **supplementary** angles *(their sum = 180 degrees)*

C + D = **90 degrees** *(C + D = 180 degrees − 90 degrees)*
Angles C and D are **complimentary** angles
Angle D = **48 degrees** *(90 degrees − 42 degrees)*

Angle E = **115 degrees** *180 degrees − (35 + 30) degrees*

Page 53

Angle A = **50 degrees** *180 − (65 + 65)* degrees
Angle B = **65 degrees** *(B = 65 because the two sides are equal)*

Angle X = **60 degrees** *(all three sides are equal)*
Angle Y = **60 degrees** *(all three sides are equal)*

Angle A = **40 degrees** *(A + 50 = 90 degrees − complimentary angles)*
Angle B = **90 degrees** *(right angle)*

Angle Z = **35 degrees** *(180 degrees − (120 − 25) degrees)*

Page 55

AC = the square root of *(8 inches x 8inches + 6 inches x 6 inches)*
    = the square root of *(64 inches squared + 36 inches squared)*
    = the square root of 100 inches squared
    = **10 inches**
AB = the square root of *(12 inches x 12 inches - 8 inches x 8 inches)*
    = the square root of *(144 inches squared − 64 inches squared)*
    = the square root of 80 inches squared
    = **8.94 inches**
Angle BAC = **43 degrees** *(angle BCA and BAC are complimentary)*

Page 56

AB is the **adjacent** side *(next to angle a)*
BC is the **opposite** side *(opposite to angle a)*
AC is the **hypotenuse** *(opposite to the right angle)*

DE is the **opposite** side *(opposite to angle B)*
DF is the **adjacent** side *(next to angle B)*
EF is the **hypotenuse** *(opposite to the right angle)*

Page 59

AB = the square root of *(8 inches x 8 inches – 4 inches x 4 inches)*
    = the square root of *(64 inches squared – 16 inches squared)*
    = the square root of *(48 inches squared)*
    = 6.928 inches

Sin of a = opposite side BC / hypotenuse AC
        = 4 inches / 8 inches
    a = arc sin of 0.5
        = 30 degrees

Cos of b = adjacent side BC / hypotenuse AC
        = 4 inches / 8 inches
    b = arc cos of 0.5
        = 60 degrees
Or
Angle b or BCA = 90 degrees – 30 degrees *(both angles are complimentary)*
        = 60 degrees

DF = the square root of *(8 inches x 8 inches + 6 inches x 6 inches*
    = the square root of *(64 inches squared + 36 inches squared)*
    = the square root of *(100 inches squared)*
    = 10 inches

Tan of a = opposite side EF / adjacent side DE
        = 6 inches / 8 inches
    a = arc tan of 0.75
        = 36.9 or 37 degrees

Tan of b = opposite side DE / adjacent side FE
        = 8 inches / 6 inches
    b = arc tan of 1.333
        = 53.1 or 53 degrees
Or
Angle b or DFE = 90 degrees – 37 degrees *(both angles are complimentary)*
        = 53 degrees

Page 60

Sin 40 degrees = opposite side AB / hypotenuse AC
Opposite side AB = hypotenuse x sin 40 degrees
            = 10 inches x 0.643
            = 6.43 inches

Page 60 continued

Cos 40 degrees = adjacent side BC / hypotenuse AC
Adjacent side BC = hypotenuse x cos 40 degrees
$\qquad$ = 10 inches x 0.766
$\qquad$ **= 7.66 inches**

BAC = 90 degrees – 40 degrees *(both angles are complimentary)*
$\qquad$ **= 50 degrees**

YXZ = 90 degrees – 45 degrees *(both angles are complimentary)*
$\qquad$ **= 45 degrees**

Sin of 45 degrees = opposite side XY / hypotenuse XZ
Opposite side XY = hypotenuse XZ x sin 45 degrees
$\qquad$ = 12 inches x 0.707
$\qquad$ **= 8.48 inches**

YZ =**8.48 inches** *(both sides are the same since the angles are the same)*

Page 61

AB = the square root of *(12 inches squared – 8 inches squared)*
$\qquad$ = the square root of *(144 inches squared – 64 inches squared)*
$\qquad$ = the square root of *(80 inches squared)*
$\qquad$ **= 8.94 inches**

Sin of a = Opposite side BC / hypotenuse AC
$\qquad$ = 8 inches / 12 inches
$\qquad$ a = arc sin of 0.667
$\qquad$ **= 41.8 or 42 degrees**

Cos of b = adjacent side BC / hypotenuse AC
$\qquad$ = 8 inches / 12 inches
$\qquad$ b = arc cos of 0.667
$\qquad$ **= 48.1 or 48 degrees**

DE = the square root of *(10 inches squared + 8 inches squared)*
$\qquad$ = the square root of *(100 inches squared + 64 inches squared)*
$\qquad$ = the square root of *(164 inches squared)*
$\qquad$ **= 12.8 inches**

Tan of d = opposite side EF / adjacent side DF
$\qquad$ = 8 inches / 10 inches
$\qquad$ d = arc tan 0.8
$\qquad$ **= 38.7 or 39 degrees**

Page 61 continued

Tan of e = opposite side DF / adjacent side EF

= 10 inches / 8 inches

e = arc tan of 1.25

= 51.3 or 51 degrees

Page 126 Assignment #17

Tan 15 degrees = opposite side / adjacent side

Opposite side = adjacent side x tan 15 degrees

Heights = opposite side + height of the entrance hole

= adjacent x tan 15 degrees + height of the entrance hole

Height at front of car = 58 inches x 0.268 + 36 inches

= 15.54 inches + 36 inches

= 51.54 inches

Height at118 inches = 118 inches x 0.268 + 36 inches

= 31.62 inches + 36 inches

= 67.62 inches

Height at178 inches = 178 inches x 0.268 + 36 inches

= 47.70 inches + 36 inches

= 83.70 inches

Height at 238 inches = 238 inches x 0.268 + 36 inches

= 63.78 inches + 36 inches

= 99.78 inches

Height at front of car = 58 inches x 0.231 + 36 inches

= 13.40 inches + 36 inches

= 49.40 inches

Height at118 inches = 118 inches x 0.231 + 36 inches

= 27.26 inches + 36 inches

= 63.26 inches

Height at178 inches = 178 inches x 0.231 + 36 inches

= 41.12 inches + 36 inches

= 77.12 inches

Height at 238 inches = 238 inches x 0.231 + 36 inches

= 54.98 inches + 36 inches

= 90.98 inches

Answers to Shooting Reconstruction Problems #1 to #15

Solutions for Shooting Reconstruction Problem #1

A.   Available Information:

Height of the muzzle of the gun above the water *(opposite side)*   = 108.5 inches
Bullet impact angle to the horizontal plane   = 6 degrees
Horizontal distance from the muzzle to the impact site in the water (adj side) = **?**

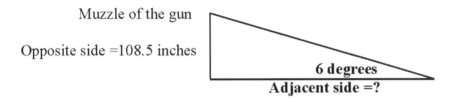

Muzzle of the gun

Opposite side =108.5 inches

6 degrees
Adjacent side =?

Available information to solve the problem:

Opposite side   = 108.5 inches
Impact angle to the horizontal plane   = 6 degrees
Adjacent side   = **?**

Only formula that could be used to solve this problem (process of elimination)

Tangent *(tan)* of 6 degrees   = opposite side / the adjacent side
Adjacent side   = opposite side/ the tan of 6 degrees
                                                                          = 108.5 inches / 0.105
Horizontal distance from the muzzle to the water   **= 1033.3 inches or 86.1 feet**

B.   Available Information:

Height of the victim's wound to her neck *(opposite side)*   = 60 inches
Angle of deflection   = 7 degrees
Horizontal distance from the deflection site to the wound *(adjacent side)*   = **?**

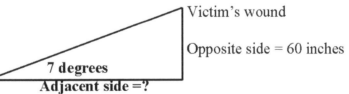

Victim's wound

Opposite side = 60 inches

7 degrees
Adjacent side =?

Available information to solve the problem:

Opposite side   = 60 inches
Angle of deflection   = 7 degrees
Adjacent side   = **?**

Only formula that could be used to solve this problem (process of elimination)

Tangent *(tan)* of 7 degrees   = opposite side / the adjacent side
Adjacent side   = opposite side/ the tan of 7 degrees
                                                                          = 60 inches / 0.123
Horizontal dist. from the water to the victim's wound = **487.8 inches or 40.7 feet**

C. No, the impact angle to the horizontal plane would have been greater than the maximum angle of 6 degrees.

D. **Available Information:**

Height of the muzzle of the gun above the water = 108.5 inches
Height of the victim's wound above the water = 60 inches
Difference in these heights *(opposite side)* = 48.5 inches or **4.04 feet**
Downward bullet impact angle to the horizontal plane, y = **?**

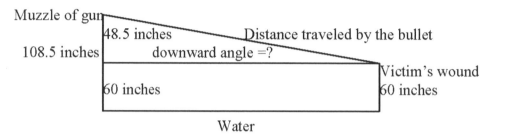

Water

Information to solve the problem:

    Opposite side *(difference in heights)* = 48.5 inches or 4.04 feet
    Adjacent side *(horizontal distance from the muzzle to the boat)* = 189.64 feet
    Downward bullet impact angle to the horizontal plane = **?**

Only formula that could be used to solve this problem (process of elimination)

Tangent *(tan)* of y degrees = opposite side / adjacent side
    = 4.04 feet / 189.64 feet
    = 0.021
    = arc tan of 0.021
Downward bullet impact angle to the horizontal plane **= 1.22 degrees**

Information to solve the problem:

    Opposite side = 4.04 feet
    Adjacent side *(horizontal distance from the muzzle to the boat)* = 189.64 feet
    Hypotenuse *(distance traveled by the bullet)* = **?**

Formula that could be used to solve this problem:

Hypotenuse squared = Opposite side squared + adjacent side squared
    = 4.04 feet x 4.04 feet + 189.64 feet x 189.64 feet
    = 16.32 feet squared + 35963.33 feet squared
    = 35979.65 feet squared
Distance traveled by the bullet *(hypotenuse)* = the square root of 35979.65 feet squared
    = 189.68 feet

Information to solve the problem:
>   Opposite side *(difference in heights)*   = 4.04 feet
>   Adjacent side *(horizontal distance from the muzzle to the boat)* = 353.32 feet
>   Downward impact angle to the horizontal plane   = **?**

Only formula that could be used to solve this problem (process of elimination)
>   Tangent *(tan)* of y degrees   = opposite side / adjacent side
>   = 4.04 feet / 353.32 feet
>   = 0.011
>   = arc tan of 0.011
>   Downward impact angle to the horizontal plane   **= 0.65 degrees**

> **Only information to solve the problem:**
>   Opposite side *(difference in heights)*   = 4.04 feet
>   Adjacent side *(horizontal distance from the muzzle to the boat)* = 353.32 feet
>   Hypotenuse *(distance traveled by the bullet)*   = **?**

Formula that could be used to solve this problem:
>   Hypotenuse squared   = Opposite side squared + adjacent side squared
>   = 4.04 feet x 4.04 feet + 353.32 feet x 353.32feet
>   = 16.32 feet squared + 124835.02 feet squared
>   = 124851.34 feet squared
>   Distance traveled by the bullet *(hypotenuse)* = the square root of 124851.34 feet squared
>   **= 353.34 feet**

> **Information to solve the problem:**
>   Opposite side *(difference in heights)*   = 4.04 feet
>   Adjacent side *(horizontal distance from the muzzle to the boat)* = 439.48 feet
>   Downward impact angle to the horizontal plane   = **?**

Only formula that could be used to solve this problem *(process of elimination)*
>   Tangent *(tan)* of y degrees   = opposite side / adjacent side
>   = 4.04 feet / 439.48 feet
>   = 0.009
>   = arc tan of 0.009
>   Downward impact angle to the horizontal plane   **= 0.53 degrees**

Information to solve the problem:
>   Opposite side *(difference in heights)*   = 4.04 feet
>   Adjacent side *(horizontal distance from the muzzle to the boat)* = 439.48 feet
>   Hypotenuse *(distance traveled by the bullet)*   = **?**

Formula that could be used to solve this problem:
>   Hypotenuse squared   = Opposite side squared + adjacent side squared
>   = 4.04 feet x 4.04 feet + 439.48 feet x 439.48 feet
>   = 16.32 feet squared + 193142.67 feet squared
>   = 193158.99 feet squared
>   Hypotenuse *(the dist. traveled by the bullet)* = the square root of 193158.99 feet squared
>   **= 439.50 feet**

Solutions for Shooting Reconstruction Problem #2

A.   Available Information:

Height of the bullet entrance hole above the ground *(opposite side)*	= 48 inches
Upward bullet impact angle to the horizontal plane	= 7 degrees
Horizontal bullet impact angle to the left when facing the driver's door	= 49 degrees

Available Information to solve the problem:

Opposite side	= 48 inches
Upward impact angle to the horizontal plane	= 7 degrees
Adjacent side *(horizontal distance)*	= **?**

Only formula that could be used to solve this problem *(process of elimination)*

Tangent (tan) of 7 degrees	= opposite side / adjacent side
Adjacent side	= opposite / tan of 7 degrees
	= 48 inches / 0.123
Horizontal distance to the truck *(adjacent side)*	= **390.24 inches or 32.5 feet**

B.   Available Information to solve the problem:

Horizontal impact angle	= 49 degrees
Hypotenuse (horizontal distance from above)	= 32.5 feet
Opposite side *(perpendicular distance to the truck)*	= **?**

Only formula that could be used to solve this problem *(process of elimination)*

Sine (sin) of 49 degrees	= opposite side / hypotenuse
Opposite side *(perpendicular distance to the truck)*	= hypotenuse x sin of 49 degrees
	= 32.5 feet x 0.755
Perpendicular distance to the truck *(opposite side)*	= **24.5 feet**

C.   Available Information:

Height of the bullet entrance hole above the ground	= 48 inches
Height of the muzzle of the gun	= 36 inches
Difference in these heights	= 12 inches
Upward impact angle to the horizontal plane	= 7 degrees

Available Information to solve the problem:

Opposite side	= 12 inches
Upward impact angle to the horizontal plane	= 7 degrees
Adjacent side *(horizontal distance)*	= ?

Only formula that could be used to solve this problem *(process of elimination)*

Tangent *(tan)* of 7 degrees	= opposite side / adjacent side
Adjacent side	= opposite / tan of 7 degrees
	= 12 inches / 0.123
Horizontal distance *(adjacent side)*	= **97.6 inches or 8.1 feet**

Available Information to solve the problem:

Horizontal impact angle	= 49 degrees
Hypotenuse *(horizontal distance from above)*	= 8.1 feet
Opposite side *(perpendicular distance to the truck)*	= ?

Only formula that could be used to solve this problem *(process of elimination)*

Sine *(sin)* of 49 degrees	= opposite side / hypotenuse
Opposite side *(perpendicular distance to the truck)*	= hypotenuse x sin of 49 degrees
	= 8.1 feet x 0.755
Perpendicular distance to the truck *(opposite side)*	**= 6.1 feet**

D.   Available Information:

Height of the bullet entrance hole above the ground	= 48 inches
Heights of the muzzle of the gun	= 39, 42 and 45 inches
Difference in these heights	= 9, 6 and 3 inches
Upward bullet impact angle to the horizontal plane	= 7 degrees

Available Information to solve the problem:

Opposite sides	= 9, 6 and 3 inches
Upward bullet impact angle to the horizontal plane	= 7 degrees
Adjacent sides *(horizontal distances)*	=?

Only formula that could be used to solve these problems *(process of elimination)*

Tangent *(tan)* of 7 degrees	= opposite side / adjacent side
Adjacent side	= opposite / tan of 7 degrees
	= 9 inches / 0.123
Horizontal distance for the muzzle height of 39 inches	**= 73.2 inches or 6.1 feet**
	= 6 inches / 0.123
Horizontal distance for the muzzle height of 42 inches	**= 48.8 inches or 4.06 feet**
	= 3 inches / 0.123
Horizontal distance for the muzzle height of 45 inches	**= 24.4 inches or 2.03 feet**

Available Information to solve the problem:

Horizontal impact angle	= 49 degrees
Hypotenuses *(horizontal distances from above)*	= 6.1, 4.06 or 2.03 feet
Opposite sides *(perpendicular distances to the truck)*	=?

Only formula that could be used to solve these problems *(process of elimination)*

Sine *(sin)* of 49 degrees	= opposite side / hypotenuse
Opposite sides *(perpendicular distances)*	= hypotenuse x sin 49 degrees
	= 6.1 feet x 0.755
Perpendicular distance for the muzzle height of 39 inches	**= 4.6 feet**
	= 4.06 feet x 0.755
Perpendicular distance for the muzzle height of 42 inches	**= 3.07 feet**
	= 2.03 feet x 0.755
Perpendicular distance for the muzzle height of 45 inches	**= 1.5 feet**

Solutions for Shooting Reconstruction Problem #3

A.　　Available Information:

Height of the center of the indentation in the driver's door　　　　= 18.25 inches
Downward impact angle to the horizontal plane　　　　　　　　= 25 degrees
Horizontal bullet impact angle　　　　　　　　　　　　　　　= 15 degrees

Information to solve this problem:

Muzzle heights	= 48, 54 and 60 inches
Height of the center of the indentation	= 18.25 inches
Differences in the heights *(opposite sides)*	= 29.75, 35.75 and 41.75 inches
Downward bullet impact angle to the horizontal plane	= 25 degrees
Horizontal distances *(adjacent sides)*	= ?

Only formula that may be used to solve these problems (process of elimination)

Tangent *(tan)* of 25 degrees	= opposite side / adjacent side
Adjacent side	= opposite side / tan of 25 degrees
Horizontal distance for the muzzle height of 48 inches	= 29.75 inches / 0.466
	= 63.84 inches

Horizontal distance for the muzzle height of 54 inches	= 35.75 inches / 0.466
	= 76.72 inches

Horizontal distance for the muzzle height of 60 inches	= 41.75 inches / 0.466
	= 89.59 inches

B.　　Information to solve this problem:

Hypotenuses *(horizontal distances calculated above)*	= 63.84, 76.72 and 89.59 inches
Opposite sides *(perpendicular distances – **green lines**)*	= ?
Horizontal impact angle	= 15 degrees

Only formula that could be used to solve these problems (process of elimination)

Sine *(sin)* of 15 degrees	= opposite side / hypotenuse
Opposite side	= hypotenuse x sin of 15 degrees
Perpendicular distance for the muzzle height of 48 inches	= 63.84 inches x 0.259
	= 16.53 inches

Perpendicular distance for the muzzle height of 54 inches   = 76.72 inches x 0.259

                                                                            = **19.87 inches**

Perpendicular distance for the muzzle height of 48 inches   = 89.59 inches x 0.259

                                                                            = **23.20 inches**

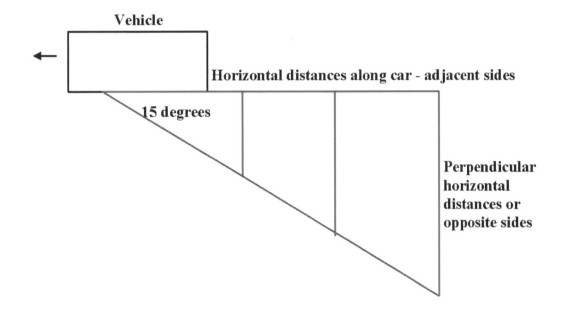

C. Information to solve this problem:

Hypotenuses *(horizontal distances calculated above)*   = 63.84, 76.72 and 89.59 inches
Adjacent sides *(horizontal distances – **blue lines**)*   = ?
Horizontal bullet impact angle   = 15 degrees

Only formula that could be used to solve these problems (process of elimination)

Cosine *(cos)* of 15 degrees   = adjacent side / hypotenuse
Adjacent side   = hypotenuse x cos of 15 degrees
Horizontal distance for the muzzle height of 48 inches   = 63.84 inches x 0.966

                                                                           = **61.67 inches**

Horizontal distance for the muzzle height of 54 inches   = 76.72 inches x 0.966

                                                                           = **74.11 inches**

Horizontal distance for the muzzle height of 60 inches   = 89.59 inches x 0.966

                                                                           = **86.54 inches**

Solutions for Shooting Reconstruction Problem #4

A.   **Available Information:**
- Height where the extended path in the opposite direction of travel
  of the projectile met the wall at the back of the assailant   = 42.5 inches
- Height of the entrance wound in the victim's chest   = 57 inches
- Upward bullet impact angle to the horizontal plane   = 15 degrees
- *Difference in these heights (victim's entrance hole and wall)*   = *14.5 inches*

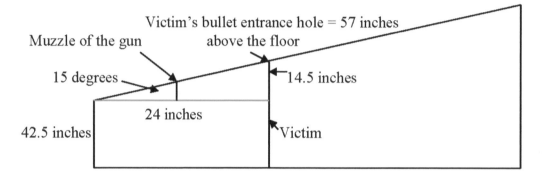

Isolating the triangle to find the horizontal distance from the wall to the wound

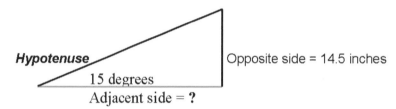

Information for solving the problem:

Opposite side	= 14.5 inches
Angle	**= 15 degrees**
Adjacent side	= ?

Only formula that could be used to solve the problem (process of elimination)

Tangent of 15 degrees	= opposite side / adjacent side
Therefore the adjacent side	= opposite side / tan of 15 degrees
Horizontal distance *(orange line)*	**= 14.5 inches / 0.268**
	= 54 inches

B.   *Isolating the triangle to find the distance from the wall to the wound*

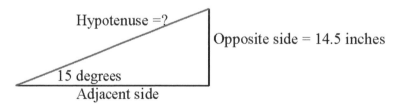

Information for solving the problem:

Opposite side	= 14.5 inches
Angle	= 15 degrees
Hypotenuse	= ?

Only formula that may be used to solve the problem (process of elimination)

Sine of 15 degrees	= opposite side / hypotenuse
Therefore the hypotenuse	= opposite side / sin of 15 degrees

Distance from the wall to the victim's chest *(blue line)* **= 14.5 inches / 0.259**

= 56 inches

C. *Isolating the triangle to find the height of the muzzle of the gun*

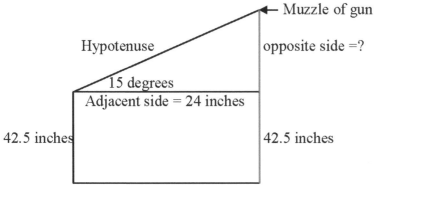

Information for solving the problem:

Adjacent side	= 24 inches
Angle	= 15 degrees
Opposite side	= ?

Only formula that could be used to solve the problem (process of elimination)

Tangent of 15 degrees	= opposite side / adjacent side
Therefore the opposite side	= opposite side x tan of 15 degrees
	= 24 inches x 0.268
	= 6.4 inches

Note: Height of the muzzle of the gun *(pink line)* = 42.5 inches + opposite side

= (42.5 + 6.4) inches

= 48.9 inches

D. *Isolating the triangle to find the distance traveled from the muzzle of the gun to the wound in the victim's chest*

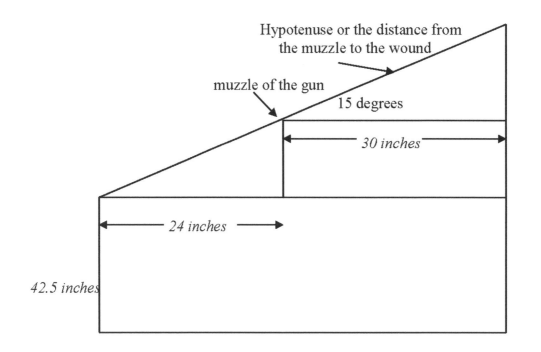

Information that may be used to solve the problem:

Adjacent side = *(54 – 24) inches =30*
inches

Angle = 15 degrees

Hypotenuse or distace traveled = **?**

Only formula that could be used to solve the problem (process of elimination)

Cosine *(cos)* of 15 degrees = adjacent side/ hypotenuse

Therefore the hypotenuse = adjacent side / cosine of 15 degrees

Distance from the muzzle to the wound = **30 inches / 0.966**

= **31 inches**

E.   *Isolating the triangle to find the horizontal distance from the muzzle of the gun to the   wound*

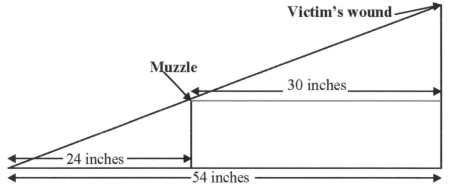

Horizontal distance from the muzzle to the wound *(brown line)* = *(54 –24) inches*

= **30 inches**

Available Information:

Horizontal distance	= 24 inches
Angle	= 40 degrees
Opposite side	= ?
Height of the bullet entrance wound in the victim	= 43 inches above the floor

Isolating the triangle to determine the height of the gun (green line)

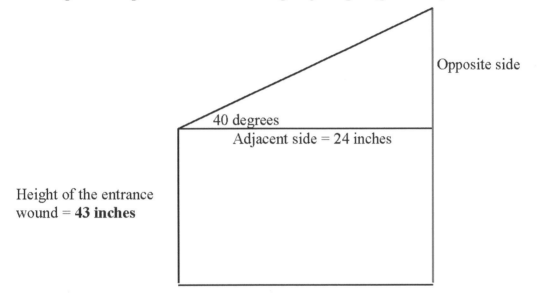

Floor

Only formula that could be used to solve the problem (process of elimination)

Tangent of 40 degrees	**= opposite side / adjacent side**
Therefore the opposite side	= adjacent side x tan of 40 degrees
Heights of the gun for horizontal distance of 2 feet	= 24 inches x 0.839
	= 20 inches

The height of the gun	*= height of the entrane wound + the opposite side*
Therefore the height for this example	= (43 + 20) inches
	= 63 inches or 5 feet 3 inches

The formula for calculating the other heights of the gun will be the same.

Height of the gun for a horizontal distance of 3 feet	**= 36 inches x 0.839 + 43 inches**
	= 73 inches or 6 feet 1 inch

Height of the gun for a horizontal distance of 4 feet	**= 48 inches x 0.839 + 43 inches**
	= 83 inches or 6 feet 11 inches

Height of the gun for a horizontal distance of 5 feet	**= 60 inches x 0.839 + 43 inches**
	= 93 inches or 7 feet 9 inches

Heights of the gun for the *50* degree angle

Note: *The tangent (tan) of 50 degrees*   = *1.192*

Height of the gun for a horizontal distance of 2 feet = 24 inches x 1.192 + 43 inches
                                               = **72 inches or 6 feet 0 inches**

Height of the gun for a horizontal distance of 3 feet **= 36 inches x 1.192 + 43 inches**
                                               = **86 inches 7 feet 2 inches**

Height of the gun for a horizontal distance of 4 feet = 48 inches x 1.192 + 43 inches
                                               = **100 inches 8 feet 4 inches**

Height of the gun for a horizontal distance of 5 feet = 60 inches x 1.192 + 43 inches
                                               = **115 inches 9 feet 7 inches**

Heights of the gun for the *60* degree angle

Note: *The tangent (tan) of 60 degrees*   = *1.732*

Height of the gun for a horizontal distance of 2 feet = 24 inches x 1.732 + 43 inches
                                               = 85 **inches or 7 feet 1 inch**

Height of the gun for a horizontal distance of 3 feet = 36 inches x 1.732 + 43 inches
                                               = **105 inches 8 feet 9 inches**

Height of the gun for a horizontal distance of 4 feet = 48 inches x 1.732 + 43 inches
                                               = **126 inches or 10 feet 6 inches**

Height of the gun for a horizontal distance of 4 feet = 60 inches x 1.732 + 43 inches
                                               = **147 inches or 12 feet 3 inches**

Isolating the triangle to determine the distance traveled by the bullet (blue line)

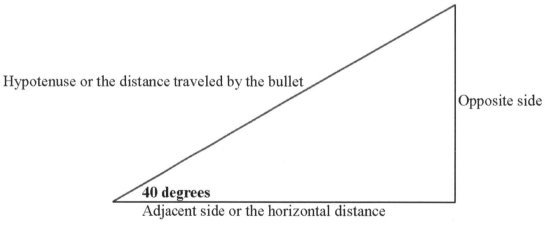

Hypotenuse or the distance traveled by the bullet

Opposite side

40 degrees

Adjacent side or the horizontal distance

Available Information:

Adjacent side *(horizontal distance)*	= 24 inches
Angle	= 40 degrees
Distance traveled or hypotenuse	= **?**

Only formula that could be used to solve the problem *(process of elimination)*

Cosine (cos.) of 40 degrees	**= Adjacent side / hypotenuse**
Therefore the hypotenuse or the distance traveled	= adjacent / cos. of 40 degrees
	= 24 inches / 0.766
	= **31 inches or 2 feet 7 inches**

The formula for calculating the other distances traveled will be the same

Distance traveled for a horizontal distance of 3 feet	= 36 inches / 0.766
	= **47 inches or 3 feet 11 inches**

Distance traveled for a horizontal distance of 4 feet	= 48 inches / 0.766
	= **63 inches or 5 feet 3 inches**

Distance traveled for a horizontal distance of 4 feet	= 60 inches / 0.766
	= **78 inches or 6 feet 6 inches**

<u>**Distances traveled for the 50 degree angle**</u>

The cosine of 50 degrees	= *0.643*
Distance traveled for a horizontal distance of 2 feet	= 24 inches / 0.643
	= **37 inches or 3 feet 1 inch**

Distance traveled for a horizontal distance of 3 feet	= 36 inches / 0.643
	= **56 inches or 4 feet 8 inches**

Distance traveled for a horizontal distance of 4 feet	= 48 inches / 0.643
	= **75 inches or 6 feet 3 inches**

Distance traveled for a horizontal distance of 4 feet	= 60 inches / 0.643
	= **93 inches or 7 feet 9 inches**

<u>**Distances traveled for the 60 degree angle**</u>

The cosine of 60 degrees	= *0.500*
Distance traveled for a horizontal distance of 2 feet	= 24 inches / 0.5
	= **48 inches or 4 feet 0 inches**

Distance traveled for a horizontal distance of 3 feet	= 36 inches / 0.5
	= **72 inches or 6 feet 0 inches**

Distance traveled for a horizontal distance of 4 feet	= 48 inches / 0.5
	= **96 inches or 8 feet 0 inches**
Distance traveled for a horizontal distance of 5 feet	= 60 inches / 0.5
	= **120 inches or 10 feet 0 inches**

Solutions for Shooting Reconstruction Problem #6

Available Information:

Height of the entrance hole	= 45.5 inches
Height of the exit hole	= 46.5 inches
Distance the projectile traveled through the wall	= 3.25 inches
Difference in these heights *(46.5 – 45.5)* inches	= 1.00 inches

Opposite side =1.0 inch

Hypotenuse = 3.25 inches

?

Information for solving the problem

Opposite side	= 1.0 inch
Hypotenuse	= 3.25 inches
Angle	= ?

A. The base of the triangle is the thickness of the wall

B. **Thickness of the wall** = square root of *(3.25" x 3.25" – 1.0" x 1.0")* = 9.56 "squared
= 3.09 inches

C. *Only formula that could be used to solve this problem (process of elimination)*

Sine?	= opposite side / the hypotenuse
	= 1.0 inch / 3.25 inches = 0.308
Angle through the wall, ?	= arc sine of 0.308
	= 17.9 or 18.0degrees

D. <u>Location of the victim</u>
Available information:

Angle	= 18.0 degrees
Height of the entrance hole in the victim's forehead hole	= 68 inches
Height of the exit hole	= 46.5 inches
Difference in these heights *(68.0 – 46.5)* inches	= 21.5 inches

Information for solving the problem:

Angle	= 18.0 degrees
Opposite side	= 21.05 inches
Adjacent side *(horizontal distance)*	= ?

Only formula that could be used to solve the problem *(process of elimination)*

Tan of 18 degrees	= opposite side / the adjacent side
Therefore the adjacent side	= opposite side / tan of 18.0 degrees
Horizontal dis. from the wall to the victim	= 2.15 inches / 0.325
	= 66 inches

E. Distance the bullet traveled from exit hole to victim's forehead

Sine of 18.0 degrees	= opposite side / the hypotenuse
Therefore the hypotenuse	= opposite side/ sine of 18.0 degrees
Distance traveled by the bullet	= 21.5 inches / 0.309 = **70 inches**

Solutions for Shooting Reconstruction Problem #7

Available information - (bullet hole #1)

Downward impact angle to the horizontal plane	= 13.0 degrees
Height of the entrance hole in the car	= 38.25 inches
Difference in the heights	= 60, 65 and 70 inches – 38.25 inches
Horizontal distances in front of the car	= ?

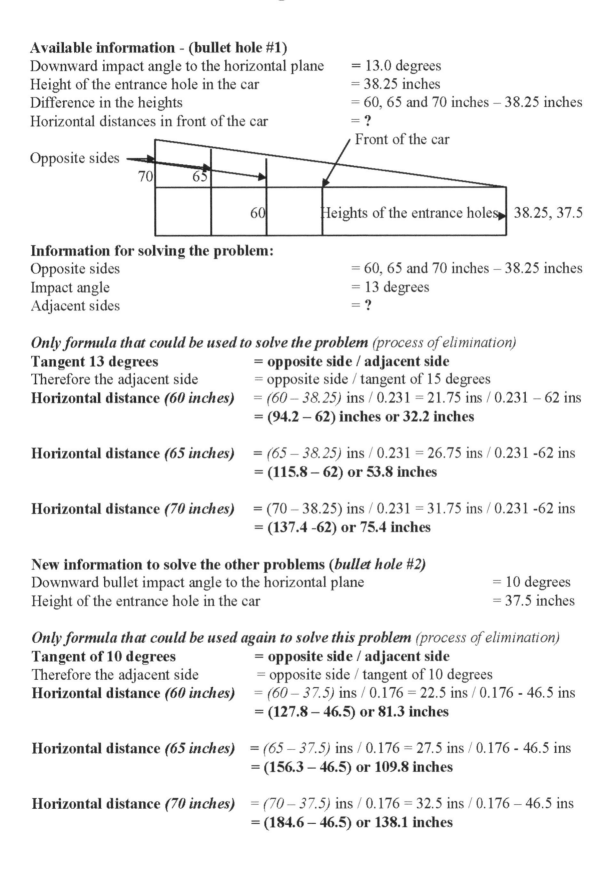

Information for solving the problem:

Opposite sides	= 60, 65 and 70 inches – 38.25 inches
Impact angle	= 13 degrees
Adjacent sides	= ?

Only formula that could be used to solve the problem (process of elimination)

Tangent 13 degrees = **opposite side / adjacent side**

Therefore the adjacent side = opposite side / tangent of 15 degrees

Horizontal distance *(60 inches)* = *(60 – 38.25)* ins / 0.231 = 21.75 ins / 0.231 – 62 ins

= **(94.2 – 62) inches or 32.2 inches**

Horizontal distance *(65 inches)* = *(65 – 38.25)* ins / 0.231 = 26.75 ins / 0.231 -62 ins

= **(115.8 – 62) or 53.8 inches**

Horizontal distance *(70 inches)* = *(70 – 38.25)* ins / 0.231 = 31.75 ins / 0.231 -62 ins

= **(137.4 -62) or 75.4 inches**

New information to solve the other problems (*bullet hole #2*)

Downward bullet impact angle to the horizontal plane	= 10 degrees
Height of the entrance hole in the car	= 37.5 inches

Only formula that could be used again to solve this problem (process of elimination)

Tangent of 10 degrees = **opposite side / adjacent side**

Therefore the adjacent side = opposite side / tangent of 10 degrees

Horizontal distance *(60 inches)* = *(60 – 37.5)* ins / 0.176 = 22.5 ins / 0.176 - 46.5 ins

= **(127.8 – 46.5) or 81.3 inches**

Horizontal distance *(65 inches)* = *(65 – 37.5)* ins / 0.176 = 27.5 ins / 0.176 - 46.5 ins

= **(156.3 – 46.5) or 109.8 inches**

Horizontal distance *(70 inches)* = *(70 – 37.5)* ins / 0.176 = 32.5 ins / 0.176 – 46.5 ins

= **(184.6 – 46.5) or 138.1 inches**

Solutions for Shooting Reconstruction Problem #8

Available Information:

Downward impact angle to the horizontal plane	= 23.0 degrees
Height of the entrance hole	= 30 5/8 or 30.625 inches
Heights of the respective locations	= 57, 74.5, 83 and 96 inches
Horizontal distances	= ?

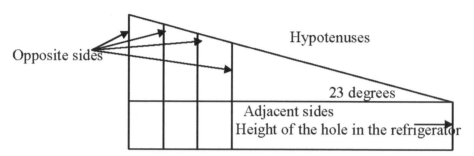

Information for solving the problems:

Impact angle	= 23 degrees
Opposite sides	= respective heights – the entrance heights
Horizontal distances	= ?

Only formula that could be used to solve the problems (process of elimination)

Tan of 23 degrees	**= opposite side / adjacent side**
Therefore the adjacent side	= opposite side / tan of 23 degrees
Horizontal distance (57 inches)	= *(57 – 30.625)* inches / 0.424
	= 62.2 or 62 inches
Horizontal distance (74.5 inches)	= *(74.5 – 30.625)* inches / 0.424
	= 103.5 or 104 inches
Horizontal distance (83 inches)	= *(83 – 30.625)* inches / 0.424
	= 123.5 or 124 inches
Horizontal distance (96 inches)	= *(96 –30.625)* inches / 0.424
	= 154.2 or 154 inches

New information for the distances the bullet would have traveled

Hypotenuses	= 68.75, 110, 130.5 and 160.5 inches

Only formula that could be used to solve the problems *(process of elimination)*

Cosine of 23 degrees	**= adjacent side / hypotenuse**
Therefore the adjacent side	*= hypotenuse x cosine of 23 degrees*
Horizontal distance (68.75 inches)	= 68.75 inches x 0.921
	= 63.3 or 63 inches
Horizontal distance (110 inches)	= 110 inches x 0.921
	= 101.3 or 101 inches
Horizontal distance (130.5 inches)	= 130.5 inches x 0.921
	= 120.2 or 120 inches
Horizontal distance (160.5 inches)	= 160.5 inches x 0.921
	= 147.8 or 148 inches

Solutions for Shooting Reconstruction Problem #9

A.   Available Information:

Height of the exit wound in the subject   = 48.25 inches
Height of the hole in the wall   = 62.0 inches
Horizontal distance along the floor   = 19 feet or 228 inches
Difference in the heights   = *(62.0 – 48.25)* inches = 13.75 inches

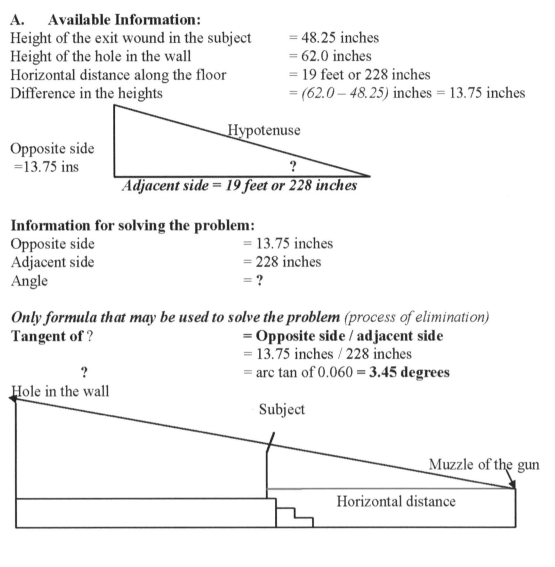

Opposite side
=13.75 ins

Adjacent side = 19 feet or 228 inches

Information for solving the problem:

Opposite side   = 13.75 inches
Adjacent side   = 228 inches
Angle   = **?**

Only formula that may be used to solve the problem (process of elimination)

Tangent of ?   = **Opposite side / adjacent side**
                                        = 13.75 inches / 228 inches
                                        = arc tan of 0.060 = **3.45 degrees**

Information for determining the location of the shooter if the projectile was not deflected:

Height of the muzzle of the gun above the ground = *30 inches*
Height of the bullet hole above the ground   = *(48.25 + 25)* inches = 73.25 inches
Difference in these heights   = *(73.25 – 30)* inches = 43.25 inches
Angle   = 3.45 degrees
Horizontal distance from the muzzle to the subject = **?**

Only formula that could be used to solve the problem (process of elimination)

Tangent of 3.45 degrees   = **opposite side / adjacent side**
Therefore the ***adjacent side***   = opposite side / tan of 3.45 degrees
Horizontal distance *(blue line)*   = 43.25 inches / 0.060
                                        = **720.8 inches or 60.1 feet**

Solutions for Shooting Reconstruction Problem #10

Height of the bullet hole above the ground   = 36.5 inches
Height of the muzzle of the gun   = 48.0 inches
Difference in these heights *(48.0 – 36.5)* inches   = 11.5 inches
Downward impact angle to the horizontal plane   = 9.0 degrees

Distance traveled (hypotenuse)

Height of the en-trance hole   Impact angle   Opposite side = 11.5 inches

Horizontal distance (adjacent side) = **?**

Hole #1 Information for solving the problem:

Opposite side *(difference in the heights)*   = 11.5 inches
Angle in question   = 9.0 degrees
Adjacent side *(horizontal distance)*   = **?**

Only formula that could be used to solve the problem (process of elimination)

Tangent of 9 degrees   = **opposite side / adjacent side**
Horizontal distance – adjacent side *(blue line)*   = opposite side / tan of 9 degrees
Horizontal distance for 48 inches muzzle height   = 11.5 inches / 0.158
     =**72.7 or 73 inches**

Horizontal distance for 60 inches muzzle height = (60 – 36.5) inches / tan of 9 degrees
     = 23.5 inches / 0.158
     = **148.7 or 149 inches**

Information to solve for the respective distances traveled by the bullet:

Adjacent side *(horizontal distance)*   = 73 inches
Angle in question   = 9.0 degrees
Distance traveled by the bullet – hypotenuse *(green line)*   = **?**

Only formula that could used to solve the problem (process of elimination)

Cosine of 9 degrees   = **adjacent side / hypotenuse**
Distance traveled for 48 inches muzzle height   = adjacent side / cos. of 9 degrees
     = 73 inches / 0.988
     = **73.8 or 74 inches**

Distance traveled for 60 inches muzzle height   = 149 inches / 0.988
     = **150.8 or 151 inches**

Hole #2 New information for solving the problem (the formulas are the same)

Height of the bullet hole above the ground $\qquad$ = 37.5 inches
Downward bullet impact angle to the horizontal plane $\qquad$ = 16.5 degrees
Horizontal distance – adjacent side *(blue line)* $\qquad$ = opposite side / tan of 16.5 degrees

Horizontal distance for 48 inches muzzle height = *(48 – 37.5)* ins. / tan of 16.5 degrees
$\qquad$ = 10.5 inches / 0.296
$\qquad$ **= 35.4 or 35 inches**

Horizontal distance for 60 inches muzzle height = *(60 – 37.5)* ins. / tan of 16.5 degrees
$\qquad$ = 22.5 inches / 0.296
$\qquad$ **= 76 inches**

Calculated horizontal distances (adjacent sides) $\qquad$ *= 35 and 76 inches*
Distance traveled by the bullet – hypotenuse *(green line)* = adj. side / cos. of 16.5 degrees

Distance traveled for 48 inches muzzle height $\qquad$ = 35 inches / 0.959
$\qquad$ **= 36.5 or 37 inches**

Distance traveled for 60 inches muzzle height $\qquad$ = 76 inches / 0.959
$\qquad$ **= 79.2 or 79 inches**

Hole #3 New information for solving the problem (the formulas are the same)

Height of the bullet hole above the ground $\qquad$ = 42.25 inches
Downward impact angle to the horizontal plane $\qquad$ = 38.1 degrees
Horizontal distance – adjacent side *(blue line)* $\qquad$ = opposite side / tan of 38.1 degrees

Horizontal distance for 48 inches muzzle height = *(48 – 42.25)* in / tan of 38.1 degrees
$\qquad$ = 5.75 inches / 0.784
$\qquad$ **= 7.3 or 7 inches**

Horizontal distance for 60 inches muzzle height = *(60 – 42.25)* in / tan of 38.1 degrees
$\qquad$ = 17.75 inches / 0.784
$\qquad$ **= 22.6 or 23 inches**

Calculated horizontal distances (adjacent sides) $\qquad$ *= 7 and 23 inches*
Distance traveled by the bullet – hypotenuse *(green line)* = adj. side / cos. of 38.1 degrees

Distance traveled for 48 inches muzzle height $\qquad$ = 7 inches / 0.787
$\qquad$ **= 8.9 or 9 inches**

Distance traveled for 60 inches muzzle height $\qquad$ = 23 inches / 0.787
$\qquad$ **= 29.2 or 29 inches**

Solutions for Shooting Reconstruction Problem #11

Available Information:

Length of all the booths (adjacent side) = *270 inches*
Distance from the above ref. wall to the bullet hole = *(47 + 51 –25.5) ins. = 72.5 inches*

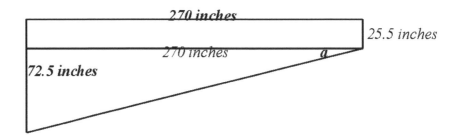

Distance from the above ref. wall to the bullet hole = (47 + 51 – 39) ins. = 59 inches

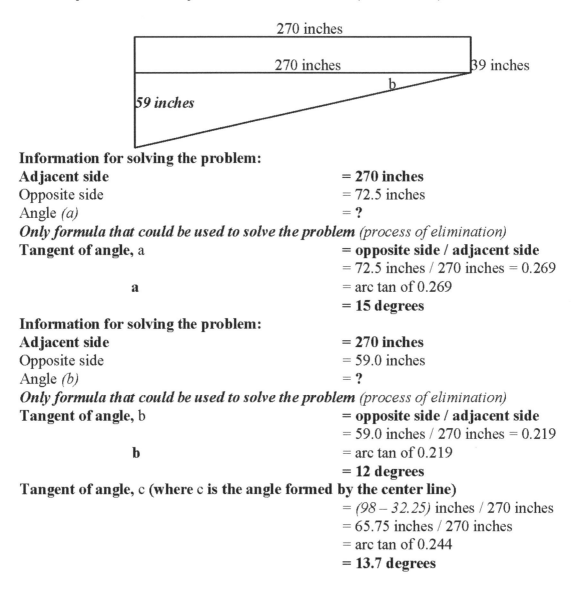

Information for solving the problem:
Adjacent side **= 270 inches**
Opposite side = 72.5 inches
Angle *(a)* = ?
Only formula that could be used to solve the problem (process of elimination)
Tangent of angle, a **= opposite side / adjacent side**
= 72.5 inches / 270 inches = 0.269
a = arc tan of 0.269
= 15 degrees

Information for solving the problem:
Adjacent side **= 270 inches**
Opposite side = 59.0 inches
Angle *(b)* = ?
Only formula that could be used to solve the problem (process of elimination)
Tangent of angle, b **= opposite side / adjacent side**
= 59.0 inches / 270 inches = 0.219
b = arc tan of 0.219
= 12 degrees
Tangent of angle, c (where c is the angle formed by the center line)
= *(98 – 32.25)* inches / 270 inches
= 65.75 inches / 270 inches
= arc tan of 0.244
= 13.7 degrees

204

The center line and 13.7 degrees will be used in the remainder of the problem. Information to solve the problem:

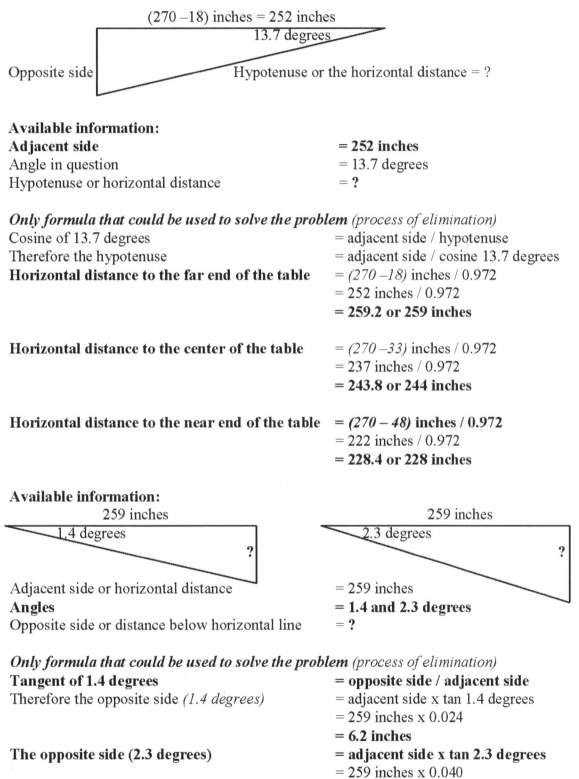

(270 –18) inches = 252 inches

13.7 degrees

Opposite side

Hypotenuse or the horizontal distance = ?

Available information:
Adjacent side	**= 252 inches**
Angle in question	= 13.7 degrees
Hypotenuse or horizontal distance	= ?

Only formula that could be used to solve the problem (process of elimination)

Cosine of 13.7 degrees	= adjacent side / hypotenuse
Therefore the hypotenuse	= adjacent side / cosine 13.7 degrees
Horizontal distance to the far end of the table	= *(270 –18)* inches / 0.972
	= 252 inches / 0.972
	= 259.2 or 259 inches
Horizontal distance to the center of the table	= *(270 –33)* inches / 0.972
	= 237 inches / 0.972
	= 243.8 or 244 inches
Horizontal distance to the near end of the table	**= *(270 – 48)* inches / 0.972**
	= 222 inches / 0.972
	= 228.4 or 228 inches

Available information:

259 inches

1.4 degrees

?

259 inches

2.3 degrees

?

Adjacent side or horizontal distance	= 259 inches
Angles	**= 1.4 and 2.3 degrees**
Opposite side or distance below horizontal line	= ?

Only formula that could be used to solve the problem (process of elimination)

Tangent of 1.4 degrees	**= opposite side / adjacent side**
Therefore the opposite side *(1.4 degrees)*	= adjacent side x tan 1.4 degrees
	= 259 inches x 0.024
	= 6.2 inches
The opposite side (2.3 degrees)	**= adjacent side x tan 2.3 degrees**
	= 259 inches x 0.040
	= 10.4 inches

The opposite side *(1.4 degrees)*	= adjacent side x tan 1.3 degrees = 244 inches x 0.024 = **5.9 inches**
The opposite side *(2.3 degrees)*	= adjacent side x tan 2.3 degrees = 244 inches x 0.040 = **9.8 inches**
The opposite side *(1.4 degrees)*	= adjacent side x tan 1.3 degrees = 228 inches x 0.024 = **5.5 inches**
The opposite side *(2.3 degrees)*	= adjacent side x tan 2.3 degrees = 228 inches x 0.040 = **9.1 inches**

Difference in the heights of bullet hole and table top = 44.25 inches − 30.25inches
= 14.0 inches

The heights of the muzzle of the gun above the table at the far end (next to the shooter)

(1.4 degrees)	= *(14 − 6.2)* inches = **7.8 inches**
(2.3 degrees)	= *(14 − 10.4)* inches = *3.6 inches*

The heights of the muzzle of the gun over the center of the table

(1.4 degrees)	= *(14 − 5.9)* inches = *8.1 inches*
(2.3 degrees)	= *(14 − 9.8)* inches = *4.2 inches*

The heights of the muzzle of the gun at the near end of the table (closer to the victim)

(1.4 degrees)	= *(14 − 5.5)* inches = *8.5 inches*
(2.3 degrees)	= *(14 − 9.1)* inches = *4.9 inches*

Solutions for Shooting Reconstruction Problem #12

A. Available information:

Height of the entrance wound   **= 53 inches**
Height of the corresponding exit wound   = 45 inches
Difference in heights   = *(53 – 45)* inches = 8 inches
Distance the projectile traveled through the body   = 22 inches

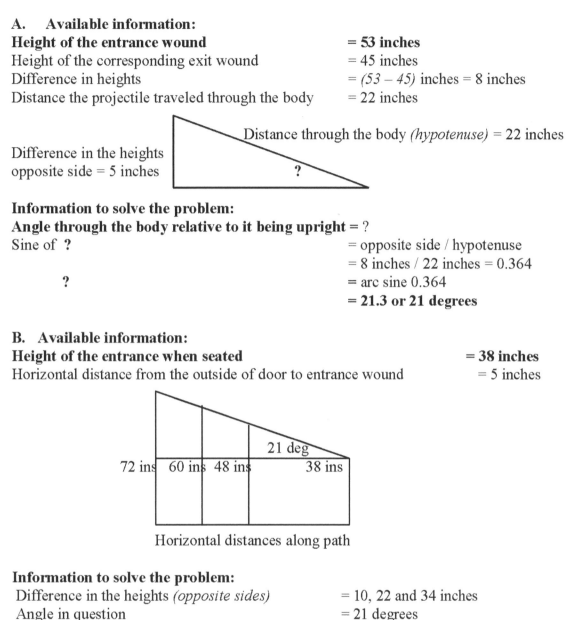

Distance through the body *(hypotenuse)* = 22 inches

Difference in the heights
opposite side = 5 inches

Information to solve the problem:
Angle through the body relative to it being upright = ?
Sine of **?**   = opposite side / hypotenuse
     = 8 inches / 22 inches = 0.364
?   = arc sine 0.364
     = 21.3 or 21 degrees

B. Available information:

Height of the entrance when seated   **= 38 inches**
Horizontal distance from the outside of door to entrance wound   = 5 inches

21 deg
72 ins   60 ins 48 ins   38 ins

Horizontal distances along path

Information to solve the problem:
Difference in the heights *(opposite sides)*   = 10, 22 and 34 inches
Angle in question   = 21 degrees
Horizontal distances (adjacent sides)   **= ?**

Only formula that could be used to solve the problems (process of elimination)
Tangent of 21 degrees   **= opposite side / adjacent side**
Therefore the adjacent side   = opposite side / tan 21 degrees
B1. Horizontal distance *(48 inches muzzle height)* = 10 inches / 0.384
     = 26 inches
B2. Horizontal distance *(60 inches muzzle height)* = 22 inches / 0.384
     = 57.2 or 57 inches
B3. Horizontal distance *(72 inches muzzle height)* = 34 inches / 0.384
     = 88.5 or 89 inches

B.   **Information to solve the problems:**

Difference in the heights (opposite sides	**= 10, 22 and 34 inches**
Angle in question	**= 21 degrees**
Distances traveled *(hypotenuses)*	**= ?**

Only formula that could be used to solve the problems *(process of elimination)*

Sine of 21 degrees	**= opposite side / hypotenuse**
Therefore the hypotenuse	= Opposite side / sine 21 degrees

C1. The distance traveled *(48 inches muzzle height)*   = 10 inches / 0.358
= 27.9 or 28 inches

C2. The distance traveled *(60 inches muzzle height)*   = 22 inches / 0.358
= 61.5 or 62 inches

C3. The distance traveled *(72 inches muzzle height)*   = 34 inches / 0.358
= 94.9 or 95 inches

D1. The horizontal distance *(48 inches muzzle height)* = *(26 – 5)* **inches = 21 inches**

D2. The horizontal distance *(60 inches muzzle height)* = **(57 – 5) inches = 52 inches**

D3. The horizontal distance *(72 inches muzzle height)* = **(89 – 5) inches = 84 inches**

E1. The impact angle would have been larger that it was.

E2. The horizontal distance would have been shorter.

E3. The distance traveled by the projectile would have also been shorter.

F1. The angle through the body would have been larger.

F2. The horizontal distance would have been shorter.

F3. The distance traveled by the projectile would also have been shorter.

Solutions for Shooting Reconstruction Problem #13

A. *Available information:*

Height of the entrance wound   = 54.5 inches
Height of the exit wound   = 51.5 inches
Distance the projectile traveled through the body   = 6.5 inches

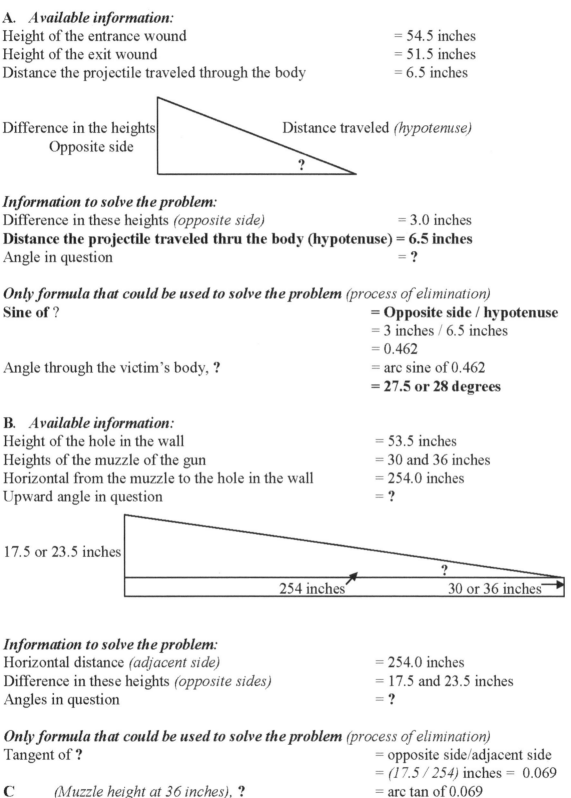

Difference in the heights   Distance traveled *(hypotenuse)*
    Opposite side
                  ?

Information to solve the problem:

Difference in these heights *(opposite side)*   = 3.0 inches
Distance the projectile traveled thru the body (hypotenuse) = 6.5 inches
Angle in question   = **?**

Only formula that could be used to solve the problem (process of elimination)

Sine of ?   **= Opposite side / hypotenuse**
                                                                 = 3 inches / 6.5 inches
                                                                 = 0.462
Angle through the victim's body, **?**   = arc sine of 0.462
                                                                 = 27.5 or 28 degrees

B. *Available information:*

Height of the hole in the wall   = 53.5 inches
Heights of the muzzle of the gun   = 30 and 36 inches
Horizontal from the muzzle to the hole in the wall   = 254.0 inches
Upward angle in question   = ?

17.5 or 23.5 inches

                          ?
254 inches   30 or 36 inches

Information to solve the problem:

Horizontal distance *(adjacent side)*   = 254.0 inches
Difference in these heights *(opposite sides)*   = 17.5 and 23.5 inches
Angles in question   = ?

Only formula that could be used to solve the problem (process of elimination)

Tangent of **?**   = opposite side/adjacent side
                                                                 = *(17.5 / 254)* inches = 0.069
C   *(Muzzle height at 36 inches),* **?**   = arc tan of 0.069
                                                                 = 3.9 degrees

Tangent *(tan)* of **?**	= *(23.5 / 254)* inches
	= 0.093
(Muzzle height at 30 inches), **?**	= arc tan of 0.093
	= 5.3 degrees

| The victim's body would have been bent over (36 inches) | = *(3.9 + 27.5)* degrees |
| | **= 31.4 degrees** |

| The victim's body would have been bent over (30 inches) | = *(5.3 + 27.5)* degrees |
| | **= 32.8 degrees** |

D. *Available information:*

Height of the exit wound	= 51.5 inches
Heights of the muzzle of the gun	= 30 and 36 inches
Angles in question	= 3.9 and 5.3 degrees

Information to solve the problems:

Difference in these heights *(opposite sides)*	= 15.5 and 21.5 inches
Angles in question	= 3.9 and 5.3 degrees
Horizontal distances *(adjacent sides)*	= **?**

Only formula that could be used to solve the problems *(process of elimination)*

| Tangent of angle | = opposite side/adjacent side |
| Therefore the adjacent side | = opposite / tan of the angle |

| Horizontal distance *(muzzle height of 36 inches)* | = 15.5 inches / 0.069 |
| | **= 224.6 or 225 inches** |

| Horizontal *distance (muzzle height of 30 inches)* | = 21.5 inches / 0.093 |
| | **= 231 2 or 231 inches** |

Information to solve the problems:

Difference in these heights *(opposite sides)*	= 15.5 and 21.5 inches
Angles in question	= 3.9 and 5.3 degrees
Distance the projectile traveled *(hypotenuse)*	= **?**

Only formula that could be used to solve the problems *(process of elimination)*

Sine of angle	= opposite side / hypotenuse
Therefore the hypotenuse	= opposite / sine of the angle
The distance traveled *(muzzle height of 36 inches)*	= 15.5 inches / 0.068
	= 227.9 or 228 inches

| The distance traveled *(muzzle height of 36 inches)* | = 21.5 inches / 0.092 |
| | **= 233.6 or 234 inches** |

E. *Available information:*

Horizontal distance	= 71 inches
Angles in question	= 3.9 and 5.3 degrees

Information to solve the problem:

Horizontal distance *(adjacent side)*	= 71 inches
Angles in question	= 3.9 and 5.3 degrees
Opposite side	= **?**

Only formula that could be used to solve the problems *(process of elimination)*

Tangent of angle	= opposite side/adjacent side
Therefore the opposite side	= adjacent side x tan of angle

The height of the exit wound *(muzzle ht of 36 inches)*	= 71 inches x 0.068 +36 ins **= 40.8 or 41 inches**
The height of the exit wound *(muzzle ht of 30 inches)*	= 71 inches x 0.093 +30 ins **= 36.6 or 37 inches**

Information to solve the problem:

Horizontal distance *(adjacent side)*	= 71 inches
Angles in question	= 3.9 and 5.3 degrees
Distance traveled by the projectile *(hypotenuses)*	= **?**

Only formula that could be used to solve the problems *(process of elimination)*

Cosine of angle	= adjacent side / hypotenuse
Therefore the hypotenuse	= adjacent side / cos. of angle

The distance traveled by projectile *(hypotenuse)*	= 71 inches / 0.998 **= 71.1 inches**
The distance traveled by projectile *(hypotenuse)*	= 71 inches / 0.996 **= 71.3 inches**

Solutions for Shooting Reconstruction Problem # 14

A. Available information:

Height of the bullet entrance hole in door = 21.25 inches
Height of the bullet exit hole in door = 20.50 inches
Difference in these heights = 0.75 inches
Distance the projectile traveled through the door = 1.625 inches

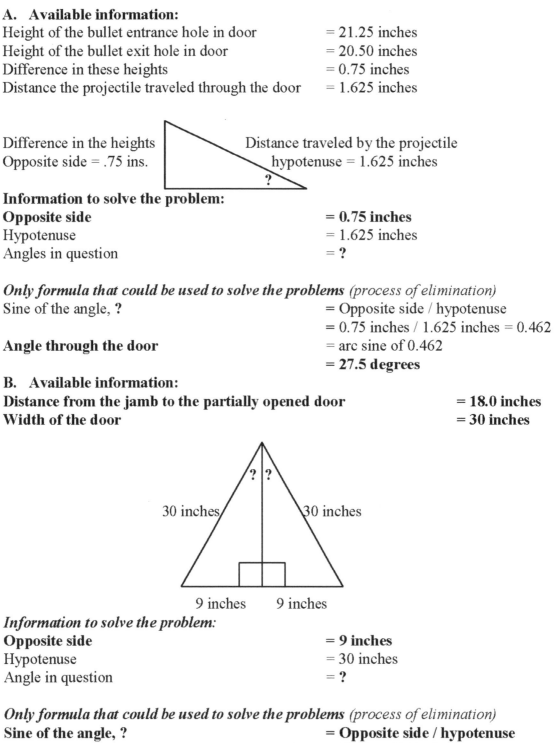

Difference in the heights
Opposite side = .75 ins.

Distance traveled by the projectile
hypotenuse = 1.625 inches

Information to solve the problem:
Opposite side = **0.75 inches**
Hypotenuse = 1.625 inches
Angles in question = **?**

Only formula that could be used to solve the problems (process of elimination)
Sine of the angle, **?** = Opposite side / hypotenuse
= 0.75 inches / 1.625 inches = 0.462

Angle through the door = arc sine of 0.462
= **27.5 degrees**

B. Available information:
Distance from the jamb to the partially opened door = **18.0 inches**
Width of the door = **30 inches**

30 inches

30 inches

9 inches   9 inches

Information to solve the problem:
Opposite side = **9 inches**
Hypotenuse = 30 inches
Angle in question = **?**

Only formula that could be used to solve the problems (process of elimination)
Sine of the angle, ? = **Opposite side / hypotenuse**
= 9inches / 30inches = 0.3
? = arc sine of 0.3
= **17.5 degrees**
Angle at which the door was opened = **(17.5 +17.5) degrees = 35 degrees**

212

C. *Available information:*

Height of the exit hole in the door	**= 20.50 inches**
Height of the bullet entrance hole in the subject's leg	= 16.0 inches
Difference in these heights	= 4.5 inches
Angle at which the projectile was traveling	= 27.5 degrees

Information for solving the problem:

Opposite side	**= 4.5 inches**
Angle in question	= 27.5 degrees
Horizontal distance	= ?

Only formula that could be used to solve the problems (process of elimination)

Tangent of 27.5 degrees	= opposite side / adjacent side
Therefore the adjacent side	= opposite side / tan 27.5 degrees
Distance from the subject's leg to the door	= 4.5 inches / 0.521
	= 8.6 inches

D. *Available information:*

Height of the exit hole in the door	**= 20.50 inches**
Angle of the projectile through the door	= 27.5 degrees

Height of the exit hole opposite side = 20.5ins

Information for solving the problem:

Opposite side	**= 20.50 inches**
Angle in question	= 27.5 degrees
Hypotenuse	= ?

Only formula that could be used to solve the problems (process of elimination)

Sine of 27.5 degrees	= opposite side / hypotenuse
Therefore the hypotenuse	= opposite side / sin 27.5 degrees
Distance traveled by projectile from door to floor	= 20.50 inches / 0.462
	= 44.4 inches

Available information

Height of the exit hole in the door	**=20.50 inches**
Angle of the projectile through the door	= 27.5 degrees

E. **Information for solving the problem:**
Opposite side   **= 20.50 inches**
Angle in question   **= 27.5 degrees**
Adjacent side   **= ?**

Only formula that could be used to solve the problems (process of elimination)
Tangent of 27.5 degrees   **= opposite side / adjacent side**
Therefore the adjacent side   = opposite side / tan 27.5 degrees
Horizontal distance from the door to the floor   = 20.50 inches / 0.521
                                                   = 39.3 inches

Available information:
Heights of the muzzle of the gun   **= 36, 42 and 48 inches**
Height of the entrance hole in the door   = 21.25 inches
Angle in question   = 27.5 degrees

Opposite side
= (36 –21.25) ins

27.5 degrees
Horizontal distance
21.25 inches

Information for solving the problem:
Opposite side   **= difference in heights**
Angle in question   = 27.5 degrees
Adjacent side   = ?
Only formula that could be used to solve the problems (process of elimination)
Tangent of 27.5 degrees   **= opposite side / adjacent side**
Therefore the adjacent side   = opposite side / tan 27.5 degrees

The horizontal distance *(36 inches)*   = 14.75 inches / 0.521
                                                     = 28.3 inches

The horizontal distance *(42 inches)*   = 20.75 inches / 0.521
                                                     = 39.8 inches

The horizontal distance *(48 inches)*   = 26.75 inches / 0.521
                                                     = 51.3 inches

F. *Only formula that could be used to solve the problems (process of elimination)*
Sine of 27.5 degrees   = opposite side / hypotenuse
Therefore the hypotenuse   **= opposite side / sine 27.5 degrees**

The distance from the muzzle to the door   = 14.75 inches / 0.462 **= 31.9 inches**

The distance from the muzzle to the door   = 20.75 inches / 0.462 **= 44.9 inches**

The distance from the muzzle to the door   = 26.75 inches / 0.462 **= 57.9 inches**

Solutions for Shooting Reconstruction Problem # 15

A.   No because the top of the driver's seat headrest was **1.0** *(one)* inch higher than the top of the driver's side *(left rear window)* rear window.

B.   The bullet that penetrated the right side of the front windshield and then impacted the top of the right windshield wiper created a fixed path relative to the trooper because it impacted two different locations of the trooper. Therefore the resultant slope of the road would not have affected the height or location of the firearm relative to the trooper. The downward slope of the road would have resulted in a change in the path of the bullet and the orientation of the trooper in the same manner.

C.   The elevation of the road at the left rear corner of the trooper relative to the right front corner of the trooper could be calculated as indicated below:

Length of the trooper	**166.5 inches**
Width of the trooper	**68.7 inches**
Length of the diagonal of the trooper	**? inches**

Formula than could be used to determine the diagonal is the Pythagorean Theorem

Diagonal squared   = the length squared + the width squared
= 166.5 inches x 166.5 inches + 68.7 inches x 68.7 inches
= 27722.25 inches squared + 4719.69 inches squared
= 32441.94 inches squared

Diagonal   = the square root of 32441.94 inches squared
= **180.12 inches**

Calculation of the elevation of the road at the left rear corner relative to the right front corner of the trooper

Resultant slope of the road	**4.5 degrees**
Distance along the road from the left rear corner to the right front corner of the trooper	**180.12 inches**
Elevation of the road at the left rear corner of the vehicle	**? inches**

Only trigonometric ratio that could be used to determine the elevation is the sine **(sin)** *ratio (process of elimination)*

Sin of 4.5 degrees   = the opposite side / the hypotenuse
Or the opposite side = the hypotenuse x the sin of 4.5 degrees
= 180.12 inches x 0.078
= **14.13 inches**

Thus the elevation of the road at the left rear corner relative to the right front corner of the trooper was approximately <u>14.13 inches</u>

D. The height of the muzzle of the firearm at the center of the front of the back support of the driver's seat which was 58 inches horizontally from the bullet hole in the front windshield when the trooper was on a flat surface could be calculated as indicated below:

Height of the bullet hole in the front windshield	**51 inches**
Downward horizontal impact angle of the bullet that penetrated the front windshield	**21 degrees**
Horizontal distance from the bullet hole in the front windshield to the center of the front of the back support of the driver's seat	**58 inches**

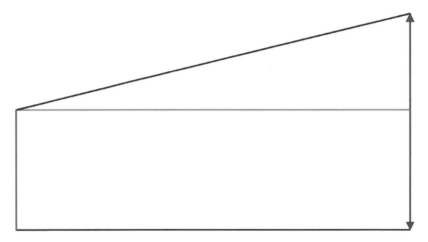

Calculation of the height of the muzzle of the firearm at the center of the front of the back support of the driver's seat

Only trigonometric ratio that could be used to determine the height of the muzzle of the firearm is the tangent **(tan)** *ratio (process of elimination)*

Tan of 21 degrees = the opposite side / the adjacent side
Or the opposite side = the adjacent side x the tan of 21degrees
               = 58 inches x 0.384
               = **22.26 inches**

Height of the muzzle of the firearm at the center of the front of the back support of the driver's seat = the height of the bullet hole + the opposite side
               = **51 inches + 22.26 inches**
               = **73.26 inches**

<u>Note:</u> *This height is greater than the height of the trooper on the level surface.*

E. The horizontal distance from the right rear corner of the back support of the driver's seat to the bullet hole in the right rear section of the headliner if the distance from the rear of the seat to the bullet hole was 47 inches and the upward impact angle to the horizontal plane was 40 degrees when the trooper was on a level surface could be calculated as indicated below:

Distance from the right rear corner of the driver's seat to the bullet hole in the right rear section of the headline near the passenger's overhead handle

47 inches

Upward impact angle of the path of the bullet that made the hole in the right rear area of the headliner **40 degrees**

Horizontal distance below the bullet's path ? inches

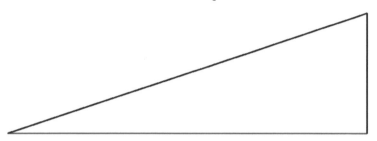

Calculation of the horizontal distance below the bullet's path

Only trigonometric ratio that could be used to determine the horizontal distance of the muzzle of the firearm is the cosine (cos) ratio (process of elimination)

Cos of 40 degrees = the adjacent side / the hypotenuse
Or the adjacent side = the hypotenuse x the cos of 21 degrees
= 47 inches x 0.766
= **36 inches**

The horizontal distance below the bullet's path was approximately 36 inches

F. Based on the two photographs of the injury to the victim's forehead, it is most likely that the bullet which grazed the victim's forehead could have deflected in an upward direction. However it is **very** unlikely that the bullet could have been deflected to the left or right based on the victim's injury thus ruling out the idea that the bullet was discharged from the outside of the left rear door window.

Trigonometric Ratios

Tangent (tan) = *length of the opposite side / the length of the adjacent side*

Sine (sin) = *the length of the opposite side / the length of the hypotenuse*

Cosine (cos.) = *length of the adjacent side / the length of the hypotenuse*

Angles	tan	sin	cos
1	0.017	0.017	1.000
2	0.035	0.035	0.999
3	0.052	0.052	0.999
4	0.070	0.070	0.998
5	0.087	0.087	0.996
6	0.105	0.105	0.995
7	0.123	0.122	0.993
8	0.141	0.139	0.990
9	0.158	0.156	0.988
10	0.176	0.174	0.985
11	0.194	0.191	0.982
12	0.213	0.208	0.978
13	0.231	0.225	0.974
14	0.249	0.242	0.970
15	0.268	0.259	0.966
16	0.287	0.276	0.961
17	0.306	0.292	0.956
18	0.325	0.309	0.951
19	0.344	0.326	0.946
20	0.364	0.342	0.940
21	0.384	0.358	0.934
22	0.404	0.375	0.927
23	0.424	0.391	0.921
24	0.445	0.407	0.914
25	0.466	0.423	0.906

Angles	tan	sin	cos
26	0.488	0.438	0.899
27	0.510	0.454	0.891
28	0.532	0.469	0.883
29	0.554	0.485	0.875
30	0.577	0.500	0.866
31	0.601	0.515	0.857
32	0.625	0.530	0.848
33	0.649	0.545	0.839
34	0.675	0.559	0.829
35	0.700	0.574	0.819
36	0.727	0.588	0.809
37	0.754	0.602	0.799
38	0.781	0.616	0.788
39	0.810	0.629	0.777
40	0.839	0.643	0.766
41	0.869	0.656	0.755
42	0.900	0.669	0.743
43	0.933	0.682	0.731
44	0.966	0.695	0.719
45	1.000	0.707	0.707
46	1.036	0.719	0.695
47	1.072	0.731	0.682
48	1.111	0.743	0.669
49	1.150	0.755	0.656
50	1.192	0.766	0.643

Trigonometric Ratios continued

Angles	tan	sin	cos
51	1.235	0.777	0.629
52	1.280	0.788	0.616
53	1.327	0.799	0.602
54	1.376	0.809	0.588
55	1.428	0.819	0.574
56	1.483	0.829	0.559
57	1.540	0.839	0.545
58	1.600	0.848	0.530
59	1.664	0.857	0.515
60	1.732	0.866	0.500
61	1.804	0.875	0.485
62	1.881	0.883	0.469
63	1.963	0.891	0.454
64	2.050	0.899	0.438
65	2.145	0.906	0.423
66	2.246	0.914	0.407
67	2.356	0.921	0.391
68	2.475	0.927	0.375
69	2.605	0.934	0.358
70	2.748	0.940	0.342
71	2.904	0.946	0.326
72	3.078	0.951	0.309
73	3.271	0.956	0.292
74	3.487	0.961	0.276
75	3.732	0.966	0.259
76	4.011	0.970	0.242
77	4.332	0.974	0.225
78	4.705	0.978	0.208
79	5.145	0.982	0.191
80	5.671	0.985	0.174
81	6.314	0.988	0.156
82	7.115	0.990	0.139
83	8.144	0.993	0.122
84	9.514	0.995	0.105
85	11.430	0.996	0.087
86	14.301	0.998	0.070
87	19.081	0.999	0.052
88	28.636	0.999	0.035
89	57.290	1.000	0.017

Squares and Square Roots
n2 means n squared and 1/2n means the square root of n

n	n2	1/2n	n	n2	1/2n
1	1	1.000	41	1681	6.403
2	4	1.414	42	1761	6.481
3	9	1.732	43	1849	6.557
4	16	2.000	44	1936	6.633
5	25	2.236	45	2025	6.708
6	36	2.449	46	2116	6.782
7	49	2.646	47	2209	6.856
8	64	2.828	48	2304	6.926
9	81	3.000	49	2401	7.000
10	100	3.162	50	2500	7.071
11	121	3.317	51	2601	7.141
12	144	3.464	52	2704	7.211
13	169	3.606	53	2809	7.280
14	196	3.742	54	2916	7.348
15	225	3.873	55	3025	7.416
16	256	4.000	56	3136	7.483
17	289	4.123	57	3249	7.550
18	324	4.243	58	3364	7.616
19	361	4.359	59	3481	7.681
20	400	4.472	60	3600	7.746
21	441	4.583	61	3721	7.810
22	484	4.690	62	3844	7.874
23	529	4.796	63	3969	7.937
24	576	4.899	64	4096	8.000
25	625	5.000	65	4225	8.062
26	676	5.099	66	4356	8.124
27	729	5.196	67	4489	8.185
28	784	5.292	68	4624	8.246
29	841	5.385	69	4761	8.307
30	900	5.477	70	4900	8.367
31	961	5.568	71	5041	8.426
32	1024	5.657	72	5184	8.485
33	1089	5.745	73	5329	8.544
34	1156	5.831	74	5476	8.602
35	1225	5.916	75	5625	8.660
36	1296	6.000	76	5776	8.718
37	1369	6.083	77	5929	8.775
38	1444	6.164	78	6084	8.832
39	1521	6.245	79	6241	8.888
40	1600	6.325	80	6400	8.944

Squares and Squares Roots continued
n2 means n squared and 1/2n means the square root of n

n	n2	1/2n	n	n2	1/2n
81	6561	9.000	121	14,641	11.000
82	6724	9.055	122	14,884	11.045
83	6889	9.110	123	15,129	11.091
84	7056	9.165	124	15,376	11.136
85	7225	9.220	125	15,625	11.180
86	7396	9.274	126	15,876	11.225
87	7569	9.327	127	16,129	11.269
88	7744	9.381	128	16,384	11.314
89	7921	9.434	129	16,641	11.358
90	8100	9.487	130	16,900	11.402
91	8281	9.539	131	17,161	11.446
92	8461	9.592	132	17,424	11.489
93	8649	9.644	133	17,659	11.533
94	8836	9.695	134	17,956	11.576
95	9025	9.747	135	18,225	11.619
96	9216	9.798	136	18,496	11.662
97	9409	9.849	137	18,769	11.705
98	9604	9.899	138	19,044	11.747
99	9801	9.950	139	19,321	11.790
100	10,000	10.000	140	19,600	11.832
101	10,201	10.050	141	19,881	11.874
102	10,404	10.100	142	20,164	11.916
103	10,609	10.149	143	20,449	11.958
104	10,816	10.198	144	20,736	12.000
105	11,025	10.247	145	21,025	12.042
106	11,236	10.296	146	21,316	12.083
107	11,449	10.344	147	21,609	12.124
108	11,664	10.392	148	21,904	12.166
109	11,881	10.440	149	22,201	12.207
110	12,100	10.488	150	22,500	12.247
111	12,321	10.536	151	22,801	12.288
112	12,544	10.583	152	23,104	12.329
113	12,769	10.630	153	23,409	12.369
114	12,996	10.677	154	23,716	12.410
115	13,225	10.724	155	24,025	14.450
116	13,456	10.770	156	24,336	12.490
117	13,689	10.817	157	24,649	12.530
118	13,924	10.863	158	24,964	12.570
119	14,161	10.909	159	25,281	12.610
120	14,400	10.954	160	25,600	12.649

CPSIA information can be obtained
at www.ICGtesting.com
Printed in the USA
LVHW071207090122
708130LV00002B/26